Closet Desire II

Closet Desire II

Erotic Dares and Other Adventures

Stephen and Susan Van Scoyoc

Authors Choice Press

San Jose New York Lincoln Shanghai

Closet Desire II
Erotic Dares and Other Adventures

Authors Choice Press
an imprint of iUniverse.com, Inc.

For information address:
iUniverse.com, Inc.
5220 S 16th, Ste. 200
Lincoln, NE 68512

Illustrated by Ray Leaning

ISBN: 0-7394-2530-7

Printed in the United States of America

Epigraph

The awareness of eroticism, unlike that of external objects, belongs to a darker side; it leads to a silent awakening.
Georges Bataille

Contents

Preface

I'd love to say *Closet Desire II* was my own idea, but it wasn't. Rather, I met up with a group of erotic writers who invented a game in which they traded erotic dares with one another. The resulting stories were often surprising, always spontaneous, and definitely sexy. There were very few rules to obey, but among them were no children, no rape, and no brutality. Some of the stories teeter on the edge of this, tempting the idea of forced or nonconsensual sex, but, with the exception of aliens from outer space—and their willing if confused victim—it will become clear that the encounters were welcome ones indeed.

We are pleased to present the first works of several writers and we think you will agree they are a talented lot whose work deserves to be in print. I had the pleasure of corresponding with the writers over the course of editing and found them to be as exciting and spontaneous as their stories. They come from all walks of life, live all over the world, and range in age from nineteen to—well—we'd rather not say!

The stories, like the writers, range from the unusual to the truly bizarre. Some are dark tales darkly told, but with an erotic mist that folds around the reader. Others are light and funny with a decidedly wicked twist. Perhaps many of these stories will touch a spot in your imagination leading you to dare your lover to fulfill your fantasy. We hope so—erotica is a dish best served warm to your lover.

Although I think you will enjoy all 22 stories there are some that have become personal favourites of mine. "Personal Space" is one of those stories that answers what many of us have been wondering for years— just what do those men and women in space really want to get up to? If the military hasn't been able to keep men and women apart how will

NASA manage when the players are orbiting the earth? James Bond may have been before his time, but sensuality in space is a foregone conclusion. "My Hanane" is a gentle, touching story of discovery between two young women travelling away from home for the first time. The experience of these two young lovers is delicate, sensitive, and powerfully erotic. Finally, "Dancing in the Dark" is a most unusual story written in a playful, punchy style and sure to have you completely drawn in by the end.

Don't take my word for it—start reading this book and I think you will find it genuine, amusing, erotic, and human. What more could you ask for?

Introduction

Most of us played "spin the bottle" when we first became aware of our sexuality—you remember—that time when something about another boy or girl made you tingle all over and want to know more? It was a thrilling excuse to explore one another's feelings—and bodies. Who can forget how our hearts raced when the bottle pointed to us and the dare was proclaimed with wicked relish?

"I dare you to...kiss Tricia...on the lips...with your tongue!"

"Ewwwww!" the girls would squeal.

We felt that same pulse quickening rush the first time we kissed our date, stroked his or her body, and when, finally, we clumsily consummated our affections. As we grew older, many of us ran out of dares—or so we thought—maybe we got chicken. Sex became routine—sensuality dulled into monotony and duty. Demoted to the end of the "things to do" list it became a late night, fast hump between the sheets and a debate about who would sleep in the wet spot. We no longer had time to play such silly games when the demands of school, work, children, in-laws, and whatever else queued up ahead of personal pleasures. Many of us promised ourselves we would take time...later. Finally, in the end, we convinced ourselves it wasn't really *that* important.

"I dare you to...touch Ricky...down there."

Ricky blushes and the group goes silent as Lisa slowly crawls over, grinning wickedly and tentatively stretching out her tiny, curious hand.

Sadly, the dull routine often takes its toll as one partner decides it *is* that important and he or she seeks excitement elsewhere—often finding it. Do we have to give up the childish exuberance that sensuality embraces? Do we really have to grow up? Or, can we save one part of childhood to share with our lovers? How well do we *really* know our lover? Would he really take a prostitute into a darkened alley, lean against a cold brick wall, and allow her lips and mouth to drive him insanely over the edge? Would she really take the stage in a stripping contest and bare all to the audience in a display of lusty abandon?

"I dare you to…reach your hand inside Nicky's blouse!"

Nicky squirms and tries to conceal her hardening nipples as David's hand brushes over the satin bra caressing her soft breasts, his fingertips eagerly and gently nudging the firm buds.

All of us marvel at the men and women who dare to jump from an airplane and gracefully float back to earth beneath a billowing canopy of nylon. We feel a touch of green envy when we see men and women our age romping down white-water rapids in a raft. We can almost feel the spray and taste the exhilaration. Instead of taking our dares, we park in front of the television and live vicariously through ever more ridiculous programs pretending to be risqué, exotic, or outrageous. We play video games with deformed female characters. All the while a thrill equal to the most exotic activities lies at our very fingertips, easily within reach. In our erotic world we can take risks that threaten to stop our hearts and then walk—or, if we're lucky, crawl—away as safely as we might an amusement park ride. We can take chances we might never take in real life and—yet—it will be as real as climbing a skyscraper without ropes and the memory will be just as delicious.

"I dare you to stop the elevator here and make love to me—NOW!"

Paul knows her moods and presses the red button. An alarm bell rings loudly, but Janet, trembling with anticipation, has already lifted her skirt, leaned over, and gripped the rails…

These are the desires that hide in the darkest corners of our closet and spring out when we least expect them. These are the stories of a small collection of writers who still make—and take—the dares. A group of writers who are living proof that the imagination is the most powerful aphrodisiac of all. Share these stories—if you dare—with your lover. See what your lover is hiding in the closet and nervously hoping you will discover—and like.

The bottle spins and clatters on the pavement as it slows down and stops.

It's your turn.

Felecia Barbaro

Personal Space

After nine weeks in space without suffering so much as a twinge of sexual desire, I suddenly began to experience an inexplicable surge of horniness. It began when I settled down in my sleeping bag for the night—that sly, oh-so-maddening itch between my legs that wouldn't go away no matter how I tried to distract myself. Even though I always told myself that I would not give in, I always ended up masturbating. If I didn't, I would lie awake for hours and in order to keep up with the rigors of living in space I had to get about eight or nine hours of sleep.

I had originally thought that I would have no problem remaining celibate through the entire six month mission. True, I had never gone that long without masturbating, but I was sure that the strange circumstances, the Spartan accommodations, and the decidedly un-sexy nature of this job would smother my libido for the duration of the mission. I had been correct, 'till now. Now I didn't know what to think.

Masturbation was the best—in fact, the only—way to deal with this increase in my sex drive. Trying to engage any crewmember in a physical relationship would be a big mistake. There were the usual problems of possible rejection and humiliation, but up here, with no way to avoid each other, those problems would be exacerbated. And assuming I found any takers, there would be no way for us to keep things discreet, not when there was so little privacy. And if we were found out, there would be the inevitable worries about the reactions from the others. There would invariably be tension or sexist accusations. I couldn't put the mission in jeopardy just for the sake of my hormonal urges. I had a job to do and the way I conducted myself up here could have an impact upon future American-Russian cooperation in space, not to mention the future of women in space. I still believed in that "Duty, Honor, Country" mantra, old-fashioned as it may be. So, I resigned myself to self-pleasuring.

When I closed my eyes and slipped my hand down the front of my sensible white cotton panties it was always Yuri, the station commander, who sprang into my fantasies. Why this happened, I didn't know. Back home I never would have looked twice at him, not because he was ugly, but because his features, from his steel-gray crew-cut to his watery blue eyes, to his somewhat weak chin, were uniformly bland. Nothing about him could be described as exciting unless you counted his brilliant scientific mind. And while I admired and respected his intellect I didn't find his personality all that engaging. His English was more than adequate, as was my Russian—but, even though he was unfailingly polite to me, we had yet to engage in a real conversation. I knew as much about him now as I had nine weeks ago. Yet in spite of all that, here I was, touching myself while fantasizing about Yuri.

My fantasy was always the same. In it I lay on top of my sleeping bag, naked from the waist down, rubbing myself furiously. I was biting my lips, trying so hard to stifle my moans and cries. Then, at the penultimate moment before orgasm, Yuri opened the door without knocking and strode into the cabin. "Alison, I need you to..." he said and then stopped dead, staring at me as I fingered myself, too far gone to stop. For some reason this mental image never failed to trigger my orgasm.

The fantasy mystified me. I had never had one like it 'till now, and I had no idea why it had so much power over me. Nor did I know why the fantasy didn't go on from there to include sexual contact between Yuri and me. It always ended with Yuri, wide-eyed and speechless, watching me finish myself off. I never imagined actually touching him or making love with him and the thought of his hands on my body left me cold. I certainly didn't feel butterflies in my tummy whenever he was near. I was as sure as I could be that sexual attraction for the man had nothing to do with this fantasy. Perhaps I was simply lonely. As the only American among a crew of Russians I was an outsider up here. No matter how polite the guys were to me, they still kept me at a distance. I tried to rationalize the fantasy by telling myself that I had subconsciously eroticized Yuri's authority over me. Somehow that explanation wouldn't wash and after struggling with the problem for a while I finally shrugged my shoulders and decided that analyzing the fantasy was silly and pointless. Might as well enjoy it and be thankful for the small diversion from the daily monotony.

Of course, sometimes it became very difficult to face Yuri during the workday. He and I sometimes had to work closely together, and on those occasions when he was rattling off a list of tasks that needed to be completed that day, I found myself drifting into my fantasy. These unbidden thoughts sent a hot shot straight to my clit and I had to squeeze my thighs together against the maddening tingle. If he ever noticed my sudden discomfort, he said nothing about it. I waited until bedtime and then satisfied myself as usual.

Things stayed exactly the same for several weeks—until last night.

I'd had an especially difficult day and I was horny and exhausted in equal measures. I lay on top of the sleeping bag, panties pulled down past my knees, head thrown back, eyes closed. My fingers were soaked as they frantically rubbed my clit. I had almost reached the part of my fantasy where Yuri burst in. I was breathing in short, harsh gasps as I felt the first small tremors that usually heralded a shattering orgasm. Then, as if from a great distance away I heard a door open and a male voice saying, "Oh, Alison, about the experiment for—holy shit!!"

My head jerked up and my eyelids popped open. Yuri stood in the doorway, his chin practically hanging on his chest, eyes bugging out. His face was turning the color of old bricks. For a moment I feared that he was going to have a heart attack right in front of me. I'd sure look cute trying to perform CPR half-naked, wouldn't I?

I gazed back at him, hand frozen between my legs, panting. I had absolutely no idea what to say to him or if I should say anything at all. I wondered if I should try to cover up in the sleeping bag—or would that make him even more uncomfortable by forcing him to acknowledge that he had trespassed upon such a private thing? What was going through his mind anyway? Did he think I was some evil, decadent Western slut? Unsure of what to do, I lay paralyzed, not daring to move at all.

Finally he managed to look away from my crotch. "I—I'm sorry," he muttered. "I should have knocked."

"It's all right, Yuri," I said. His embarrassment was somehow very moving.

"You do get kind of lonely up here," he said, still looking at the floor.

"Yes." I raised my butt up a little and grabbed the waistband of my panties, preparing to pull them up.

"No!" Yuri's voice startled me and I glanced up at him. He was looking at me, even though his face was still flushed. "Don't cover yourself up on my account," he said.

I let go of the waistband and lay back. "Okay."

He glanced at the brown bush that covered my mound. "I've never seen a woman do…that before," he murmured. His face turned an even darker shade of red.

My clit tingled a little at those words. "Really?"

"Really."

He was biting his lip now, staring openly at my pussy. I glanced at the crotch of his blue coveralls—yep, there it was—a bulge.

"Yuri," I said softly.

I could see the effort it cost him to take his eyes from my pussy and meet my gaze.

"Yes?"

"Would you like to watch me…finish?" The itch was back, stronger than ever now.

He licked his lips, raked his fingers through his bristly crew-cut. "Would I? Oh yes, definitely!"

He grinned, showing a lot of teeth.

"I don't believe this—my whole life I've been dreaming about watching a woman pleasure herself! Who knew I'd find her in outer space?"

I chuckled. "Is that your secret fantasy, Yuri?"

He dropped his gaze and nodded. For a moment he reminded me of a little boy, although he had to be at least forty-five years old. Again I felt moved.

"All right, then," I said. "I'll do it, but on one condition. Well, two, actually."

"Yes, anything." He looked up at me again, his face almost puppy-like in his eagerness.

"First close the door. We don't want the whole crew watching this."

"Oh! Yes, of course!" He reached behind him and shut the door. "And the second condition?"

"The second condition is that you must play with yourself too, at the same time, because I've never seen a man do it. How does that sound?"

For a second I wondered if I had gone too far, but the excited look on Yuri's face settled that question for me. "Sure. I'd love to. I—I was going to do it tonight anyway."

He reached into the pocket of his coveralls and pulled out a condom. "Zero gravity—you know what happens," he said. I nodded.

He hurriedly unzipped his coveralls and then pulled out a very impressive looking circumcised cock. It looked to be about seven inches long and was quite fat. I quickly revised my earlier evaluation of Yuri as possessing no exciting physical qualities. He was aware of my gaze, but his embarrassment seemed to have vanished. Carefully he unrolled the condom and put it on. When it was in place, he looked at me and gave me a thumbs-up, just as if we were performing some experiment.

"All right then. Get ready."

I spread my legs to give him an unobstructed view then began running my index finger all around my pussy lips. He grunted, then took hold of his cock and worked his hand up and down. Neither of us spoke as we caressed ourselves. His eyes were locked onto my moving fingers and I couldn't stop watching the motion of his jerking hand. There was no sound apart from our heavy breathing and the occasional squishing noise from my pussy. The excitement took hold of me again, but it was sharper this time. Waves of pleasure were radiating out from my clit, all through my belly.

Yuri seemed powerfully excited. His face and neck were flushed a deep red and his mouth gaped open. I wondered if his cock was as red as his face, but the condom and his quickly moving hand made it difficult to tell. His knees were shaking a little and that more than anything sent me over the edge. I somehow managed not to scream as the orgasm tore through my belly although I did make a few unladylike grunting noises. Yuri's eyes bugged out even more as he watched me tense up and midway through my pleasure I saw his face tighten as his own climax occurred. His eyes squeezed shut and he made a few strangled noises.

When the last tingles had died away, I collapsed and grinned up at Yuri. He wobbled a little on his feet and had to reach out to the wall in order to steady himself. "My god," he murmured, wiping sweat off his forehead with his free hand. "That was wonderful."

"I enjoyed it too," I said.

Yuri blushed again and looked away.

"Thank you," he muttered. "I ought to go now. I have to dispose of this."

He carefully removed the condom and held it a little away from himself, as if it contained something mildly unpleasant. He glanced back at me, gave me a shy little smile and said, "Have a good night and pleasant dreams."

"You too," I replied, but he was already walking out the door.

Today Yuri was as cordial to me as always. He acted as if last night never happened and I was happy to play along. We were so busy that I couldn't have asked him about it even if I wanted to. But a few minutes ago, as I was saying my goodnights to the crew, I thought I saw a glint in his eye. It might have been my imagination, but it sent another tingle to my crotch.

So here I am, on top of the sleeping bag, panties around my ankles. I've been stroking myself for about ten minutes now, just keeping myself primed. I want to be ready in case Yuri barges in again. I've come up with another fantasy.

L.M.H.

My Hanane

We were between Paris and London when Hanane and I first met. We were on our way to France on a rusty, antiquated tour bus—she, to visit her father, I to see the world—and as luck would have it, we ended up seatmates. Being that I was one of the first passengers to board, I had gotten a great seat. I was hoping to sleep my way to Paris, so after getting comfortable, I immediately put my backpack in the chair next to me to discourage people from sitting there. It worked perfectly until Hanane boarded the bus. She happened to be the last passenger to get on and so seats were scarce. I looked around hoping, praying that there would be another seat available, any other seat available, but there was not one to be had.

"Damn!" I sighed, "So much for that."

I quickly moved my bag to the under-seat storage area to make room for my unwanted guest. I watched her as she approached. She was an attractive girl, probably about my age and wearing a small, blue, cotton, spaghetti strap shirt and a pair of short denim shorts. She smiled at me and I could tell she was going to be a talker. I tried to avoid smiling back, but unfortunately I just couldn't help it. The woman had a warm, infectious smile that could light up a funeral.

"I am very sorry," she said shyly as she sat down. "I like to have a seat to myself, too. It is busy during the summers, though. Do not worry, I will not bother you."

"Oh no, uhh...don't worry about it. I don't mind if you sit here...really!" I responded, feeling more than a little guilty.

She smiled a little less brightly this time, and a little more knowing.

"Sure, sure," she laughed. "I looked at your face when you realized I was going to have to sit here. You looked like you were going to kill me!"

It was my turn to laugh, as I knew it was true.

"I'm sorry, I'm just tired. I've been traveling for forever it seems like and I'm so worn out."

"I understand," she said nurturingly. "By the way, I am Hanane."

"I'm Marie," I replied, accepting her handshake.

It was going to be hard not to like this girl, I thought. She had all the manners of a proper English woman, yet all the charm of a youthful French maid. Her smile, her laugh, her eyes—all so good-natured and inviting. And then she was just so pretty. I had thought she was attractive from afar, and now up close there was no denying it. The girl was gorgeous—and a complete opposite of me. Where I was a mere 5'0", she was a statuesque 5'9". Where my breasts were a little too small, my hips a little too straight, and my tummy a little too soft, hers were runway model perfect. Where I had long, dark, curly hair that hung loosely down my back, she had long, wavy blonde hair that was pulled casually up into a ponytail. Where I had dark, sultry, seductive eyes, she had pale, open, friendly blue ones. Where I spoke in my dirty, uncultured American way, her words carried with them an indelible French accent that just reeked of fine culture and taste.

"So Marie, you are touring Europe, I suppose?"

"Yes, for about a month now. My parents wanted me to go to college right away, but I didn't want to. I wanted to experience the world, not learn about it in textbooks, you know?"

Hanane laughed at that.

" Yes, I know!" she agreed. "That is what my mother wanted me to do! She wanted me to go to school and be a doctor. That is why I am coming back to Paris, to live with my father. He's much more... umm... how do you say?...liberal than my mother."

"Oh, I see," I responded. "So what are you going to do then?"

"I am going to paint!" she said with a smile.

That smile. It was just catchy and I found myself smiling right along with her. After that, we talked like old friends; we just passed the time reliving memories from the past and dreaming dreams of the future. When we eventually arrived in Paris we got off the bus laughing and giggling like the giddy teenagers we were.

She was showing me around later that same evening when she suggested we stop for dinner. My stomach growling, I didn't hesitate to agree. We decided to stop at the first quaint little café that we came across. I ordered tea and a *Croque Monsieur*, only after asking Hanane what it was. If I'd learned anything on my travels, it was to know what I was ordering.

We ate casually and talked some more. When we were done, Hanane suggested that we rest in the park until the sun had set some. I said yes immediately. My tiredness had receded as I got to know Hanane, but it had returned now that we had eaten.

We chose a quiet, secluded spot just beneath a big, tall, old oak tree in a far corner of the park. Hanane pulled a blanket from her bag and spread it across the ground. We both kicked off our shoes and then she sat down, crossing her legs and patting the ground next to her, motioning for me to sit there. I did.

"Sleep now," she said with a sigh. "Sleep now."

And then with that, she leaned over and kissed me softly on the cheek. Her kiss could have been any kiss between friends, but her lips caressed my flesh just a little too long and a little too hard to have been a purely innocent one. I didn't really know what to make of it—it felt so sweet and so tame, but at the same time it felt so naughty and so sensual.

"Sleep sweetie," she said, "I will wait for you," and motioned for me to lie on her lap.

Obeying, I rolled over onto my side to rest my head on her crossed legs. Contented, I closed my eyes and let my mind drift. I was almost asleep when I felt her hands start to softly stroke my hair. Her attention was so nice, so soothing, so very suggestive. My nipples were hardening in response and a pleasant ache was developing at my center. Before I knew it, any intentions I had of sleep were gone from my mind. Now, all I could concentrate on were the hands that were running through my hair and the sharp tingles of excitement that they were causing. I had forgotten exactly where I was and who I was with. Hanane must have sensed my excitement because her hands gradually moved lower and lower. She caressed my face and my neck and then lightly grazed the exposed skin just above my breasts. I couldn't help but sigh as my body involuntarily arched to meet her touch.

"Do you like this, Marie?" Hanane whispered in my ear.

I could only moan in response.

Her hair, which she had apparently been let down from her ponytail, fell in front of my face. It smelled so sweet, so feminine and it turned me on more than even her loving caresses had.

My head was now nestled comfortably in the little crevice between Hanane's legs and I was suddenly aware of her gently rubbing her crotch against it. Her breathing had deepened now and it matched, almost exactly, the movement of her hips.

This feels so incredible, I thought. I'd never been with a woman before—never even considered it—but I knew without a doubt that I had to have Hanane. The way she was pressing her hips against me and the way she was touching me—so soft—was all so very, very erotic. I wanted to get up and kiss her, to taste her succulent lips, but then I remembered where we were.

With this in mind, I picked my head up from her lap, stuttering that we were in a public place, that we should go somewhere else.

"Sssh. Look around Marie."

I did. To my amazement there was hardly anyone in sight and night had fallen. It was dark now. Either it had been longer than I had thought or I had drifted off to sleep without realizing it.

Knowing my thought, Hanane quickly solved my dilemma.

"You were asleep, Marie. Everybody left..."

And then I couldn't help myself anymore. I was burning up inside and her ripe, full lips were calling to me. I leaned over and pressed my lips to hers.

It was like nothing I'd ever experienced before. Her kiss was so soft, so slow, so sweet, so utterly feminine that I literally melted in her mouth.

"Mmm," I moaned into her. "Touch me."

I could feel her smile as her hands immediately obeyed, finding their way to my breasts, fondling them through the thin t-shirt I was wearing.

"You are so sexy, Marie. I'm glad I got to sit next to you. I wanted to make love to you the first moment I saw you in the station," she breathed.

Her words set my body on fire. My mouth left her face and traveled down to nuzzle her neck. I kissed my way lower to that soft, sexy cleft between her shoulder blades. I love that part of a woman...it's just so graceful. But I couldn't stop there, I was hungry and I wanted to lick, to bite, to devour every single part of her. I brought my hands up to her shoulders and pushed the thin straps of her shirt down over her shoulders. My breathing ceased as the shirt fell slowly down around her taut stomach and her braless breasts were finally revealed to me. They were small, but firm and perfectly round. Her pretty, pink nipples were erect from the cool air and I leaned over to warm them in my mouth. She held me to her, her hand behind my head pressing my face insistently into her chest.

"Yes Marie, like that...just like that...aahhhhh."

Her words kept me going, my mouth never faltering at her breasts. I unbuttoned her denim shorts, pushed them down her long, silky legs, and left her wearing nothing but a pair of red silk panties.

"You are so beautiful, Hanane," I said, breathless.

At this point, she was already so flushed that I couldn't imagine her getting any redder, but she did. Surprisingly shy, she blushed, her cheeks becoming engorged with blood, at my compliment.

She looked so sweet and naïve at that moment—so young, so pretty, so very, very innocent—that I wanted to just take her in my arms and hold her and cuddle her and love her forever. Indeed, I think I could have had I not suddenly felt Hanane's hands tugging urgently at my shirt, trying to pull it up and over my head. Laughing in response, I snapped out of my reverie and helped her. When we finally succeeded in removing and discarding the piece of clothing, I lowered my body down on top of hers. Like her, I wasn't wearing a bra and so our breasts were immediately pressed against each other. It felt so nice, flesh against flesh, woman against woman.

"Have you ever been with a woman before, Marie?"

"No, I… I haven't."

"Let me teach you then, my sweet friend," she whispered.

This was not just sex, I thought then as Hanane nuzzled my neck, this was pleasuring another person because you cared about them; this was making love.

She rolled me over so that I was on my back and began removing my jeans. Her mouth settled on my breasts, kissing and sucking and nibbling them to no end. When she finally got my pants off, her tongue made its way down to my smooth, pale stomach and teased at my belly button for a long while before eventually journeying further down to just above my white, cotton panties.

"Mmm…God, Hanane, please don't stop."

She chuckled and replied, "Not so fast, sweetie."

She then continued further down my body, skipping my pelvis and starting again at my thighs. She softly licked the sensitive inner parts, gently nuzzling the damp crevice there, before moving lower still to my calves. She kneaded them as she went, squeezing the skin and massaging the muscles.

For the second time, she asked, "Do you like this, Marie?" and for the second time, all I could do was moan in response.

She just laughed again and then surprised me by licking the arch of my foot and then moving on to each one of my toes. I gasped in shock at all the wonderful sensations she was causing. I had never had this done before and it felt simply amazing, but then—just as I was really getting into it—she stopped.

"Don't stop, Hanane, pleeeeeeeaaaaase don't stop."

"Don't worry, my sweet Marie, I'm not going to."

And with that she immediately planted her face firmly between my legs, licking and nibbling at my moist, panty-covered pussy.

My hips moved upward to push her face further, harder into me, but then, to my dismay, she stopped again.

I sighed in disappointment, but Hanane quieted me.

"It'll get better," she breathed.

She then slipped my panties down to my ankles and slowly teased her way back up my legs. I was writhing on the blanket now and could feel my wetness seeping from my pussy.

"Please baby, please stop teasing me and eat me. Just eat me!" I cried. She was driving me insane!

Finally, she did what I asked. She placed her tongue flat on my wet pussy, covering the lips, and then began licking up and down from just above my slit to that sensitive stretch of skin just below my vagina. She kept this up for awhile, but eventually she found my clit and concentrated on it, never allowing her tongue to lose contact with it. I tried to be quiet, to keep my pleasure in, but when she started fingering me, I just lost it.

"Ohhh yes, Hanane!" I screamed. "Oh, mmm, that's so fuckin' good! Damn, it feels so good…oh yesss."

I know I kept screaming, but the rest was just incoherent ramblings. I could hear the slurping sounds as she sucked up my juice and the wet little squishing sound as she fingered my cunt. They were turning me on so much…but then just as I thought it couldn't get any better, Hanane shoved a finger roughly up into in my ass. That was it. That was all I could take and my body just exploded. My thighs clenched around her head and my hips pumped up and down relentlessly as wave after wave of pleasure shot through me. When it was finally over, Hanane moved up my body and kissed me hard, letting me taste myself on her soft, full lips.

"Now Marie, please…" she begged. "Make me feel good."

Not needing any urging and figuring she'd had enough teasing making love to me, I went straight for her pussy. I quickly removed her silky panties and gasped audibly as I got my first glimpse of a woman's pussy. Hanane's was trimmed neatly, with hair only above her slit. So pretty, I thought, just like a flower.

A bit unsure of myself, I lapped at it only tentatively at first. The taste was a little tangy and I jumped as a result, but then I grew accustomed to it. Being that I didn't know quite what to do, I just licked her like she'd licked me. I started by first laving her whole pussy with my tongue, not opening the lips, just making my tongue flat along the outside. Then, I opened her lips with my hands. Her rather large clit was peeking out from its hood and I gently flicked at it with my tongue. Hanane's body jumped and she screamed in response. Encouraged, I continued to play with her clit while I slipped two fingers into her hot, waiting pussy.

"Mmm," she moaned. Her body was shaking and her breath was coming very rapidly now. "Put your finger in my ass, Marie. I love that…please…"

I was a bit hesitant, but I wanted so desperately to please her, so I licked a finger and worked it into her ass.

"Yes Marie…Oh God!"

Her hands were at her tits now, kneading and pulling at them violently. Damn, she was so hot! She was working herself into a frenzy and I couldn't help but go along with it. I decided that if she loved to have her ass fingered, like me, she'd love to have it licked, like me. I took my tongue from her clit and moved it lower to lick her pink, puckered asshole. She obviously loved this, as she let loose a shrill scream and began creaming all over my face in orgasm.

"Yes, Yes, Yessss!! Oh God Marie...Marie!"

I continued to finger her tight, dripping pussy and tongue her pretty little asshole until I knew that her orgasm had subsided and her body had finally gone limp. I moved up and kissed her full on her lips once more, this time tasting both of us, together. Pulling away and moaning softly, she brought her legs up and crossed them again, just like they were before and then again guided my head to rest in her lap.

"Sleep now," she said with a sigh. "Sleep now."

Stephen Van Scoyoc
The Black Bull

Well, here I was again in this forlorn, dreary northern Yorkshire village for yet another pointless meeting of the board of directors of a non-profit museum trust. The youngest of the directors at forty-two, I was the outsider—the unknown factor—and most members had been slow to warm up to my presence and strong opinions. Unlike the other members who were mostly retired locals with ties to the museum and its employees, I was a business man—an American capitalist—with a successful and profitable business in London. I didn't know when I was nominated how appalling the finances were or I would have run the other way screaming in terror. How could I suspect? The chairman had said "we are a rich charity" and plans were well underway to build a new £2,000,000 museum. When I reviewed the accounts for the first time I was stunned. A few quick but careful calculations estimated the charity would be bankrupt in less than three years.

Today I had once again voiced my concerns and recommended a course of action that included staff cuts and raising admission prices. The others turned from me, shunned me, and began talking about selling mince pies and mull wine to raise money and sending post by second class instead of first. They seemed to have no grasp of the fact that £50 raised by a bake sale wouldn't touch an £80,000 a year deficit. In exasperation I turned my attention to more entertaining things—like Chloe.

Chloe was a student intern in the second year of her post graduate studies in fine arts at a nearby university. We often employed students like Chloe to help out around the museum. Today Chloe was filling in as secretary and taking minutes of the meeting. She was definitely the most interesting person there. Young and vivacious not to mention terribly attractive in the best of English ways. Chloe looked up from her notes, caught my eye, and smiled. I smiled back.

I had met Chloe a few weeks earlier and been charmed by her intelligence and wit. Her dark brown eyes flashed with passion and hinted at an Asian flavour that was common in this part of England. Always meticulously groomed, her dark hair was now cut in a bob and fell short upon the white skin of her neck. Like many young English women she was petite and very slender which accentuated her curves in the most delicious of ways. Today she was dressed in a black, close-fitting ribbed jumper, a short black and white checked skirt, and the traditional stockings and black shoes of her generation. I never quite figured out these Yorkshire women when it came to clothes. Even when the wind swirled in off the moors and the snow blanketed the crags, the women wore the barest minimum of clothing.

My attention was suddenly broken when a question was directed at me. I apologised and asked the chair to repeat the question. Quickly answering the question, my attention fell back upon watching Chloe as she bent over her notes and squirmed occasionally in the hard chair. When the meeting was over I didn't wait around but headed out into the blustery cold of the cobbled streets and went straight to the Black Bull, a pub with rooms on the upper floor.

I was the only member staying in the Black Bull because it was too expensive for the rest of the members. The charity only allowed £18 for a room which, even in this remote village, only covered the cost of a small room in somebody's house with a shared toilet down the hall and a shower with an anaemic spray. I preferred the largest room in the Black Bull, at £70, with its centuries old wooden beams, leaded windows, and grand view of the moors beyond the village. I had travelled here by first class on the train which, of course, also exceeded the allowances offered by the charity. I didn't mind paying the extra if I was going to be kept away from my comfortable home in southern England.

I entered the smoke-filled pub and welcomed the warm blast of air. It was already full of locals gossiping and drinking down pint glasses of northern stout. As I passed the bar I asked Carol, the landlord's daughter, to bring a glass of port to my room. Carol always looked surprised when I mentioned her name. I usually remember people's names and any little titbits they tell me about themselves. It pays off later when you want something special—like a glass of port brought to your room.

Finally warmed by the port and the small peat fire crackling in my fireplace I decided to return to the pub below and have tea. Carol dropped what she was doing to come and take my order. She recommended the venison in current sauce and new potatoes, which I graciously accepted. I asked for a pint of Caffrey's to drink. Carol didn't yet know where I would be sitting, but I knew that she would find me when it was ready. She always did.

I looked around for a place to sit and behind a massive pillar of timber I saw Chloe! She was sitting with one of the locals, a young man about her own age although he looked a bit rough for a woman of her poise. She didn't seem to notice me so I walked over to her table to say hello. She looked up at me with a quizzical expression and I began to feel a bit foolish.

"Chloe?" I asked a bit tentatively. Surely I didn't make a mistake.

Her face softened into a bright smile and then a laugh.

"Kirsty—I'm Kirsty—you mean my sister Chloe!"

Twins! I thought to myself. Of course. How delicious!

Just then I heard the door to the loo creak open and Chloe walked over with a big grin on her face. Obviously this happened all the time. Introductions were made all around and we moved to a larger table. They had just finished their meal and I had expected them to move on, but Chloe told me they were stranded. The roads had grown icy after the low winter sun had disappeared and they couldn't even make it to the next town, only three miles away, where they lived. They were waiting for an opening at one of the B&Bs in town, hoping that the weather would result in a cancellation at one of the fully booked inns.

The young man, Simon, was also stranded. He and Kirsty had been friends in school until he turned sixteen and left school to work on a nearby farm. He was a boorish lout who talked about nothing but football. I thought Kirsty and he might be an item, but as he put away the lager it became clear that she was simply being polite to an old school chum.

Kirsty and Chloe were, like many young English people, deeply interested in America and in between bites of my food I answered their questions and told tales of life in the States. Simon seemed annoyed and never missed a chance to have a dig at the Americans for one thing or another. We all humoured him.

Although they were identical twins they were anything but identical. Kirsty had just finished a degree in literature and was a bit of the wild one. She had just returned from a summer of touring in Europe before trying to look for work. Her eyes gleamed with mischief. Still, the two women seemed to adore one another and enjoyed teasing each other about their own exploits.

Kirsty had just begun talking about how she wanted to fly to Las Vegas and win big at cards when Carol arrived to clear off the table. We looked around and most of the crowd had already drifted away. It was nearly 10.30 and the bar would only be serving until 11.00 so most had taken one last drink and stumbled on home in the cold. We had been so engrossed in our talk that the twins had forgotten to go out looking for a room Now all the B&Bs were shuttered up and preparing to sleep. I suggested they could all stay in my room and looked at Carol for her approval. She looked at Chloe and Kirsty then gave a knowing smile to me and said it would be alright.

Suddenly Kirsty blurted out "let's play cards!"

I hadn't played cards since my time in the Navy, but I turned and asked Carol if she could bring a deck. Maybe I would remember how. Carol was back in a flash with a deck of worn cards as well as another round of drinks for us. Kirsty was on the edge of her seat, looking very sneaky as we waited for Carol to set down the glasses and leave. When Carol walked away Kirsty leaned over and said let's play "strip and dare" poker. In spite of myself an electric excitement streaked through my body.

"Right here?" I asked. There were still people in the pub, but we were partially hidden in the alcove where our table was. Of course I was thinking excitedly about the stir it would cause if we started stripping out of our clothes right there in the pub. Kirsty was ready for that. Chloe just looked on in knowing amusement at her sister's antics.

"It'll be fun—we'll take off our underwear first and with that she coyly looked around, reached under the table, wriggled her hips a bit, and gleefully dropped her knickers on the table!"

"KIRSTY!" Chloe scolded.

Even Chloe was a bit surprised but I thought it was beginning to look like real fun. I started shuffling the cards.

Simon had suddenly become surprisingly quiet, but I think the prospects of seeing Kirsty or Chloe without clothes overcame his reservations and in a gesture of mock machismo he agreed to the game. We all anted up with the easy stuff, a sock here, a belt there, and one of Chloe's lace top stockings. I was beginning to feel a bit wicked.

Chloe lost the first hand. Maybe I was wrong about Kirsty being the wild one. Chloe lifted up her jumper and unfastened her bra. Then she deftly pulled her arms into the jumper, slipped the straps off her shoulders, and dropped her bra in the middle of the table. I felt my cock shift in my trousers. Just the thought of her naked breasts being hugged by the clingy jumper and her tender nipples grazing the rough fabric was distracting me from the game. I lost the hand.

Since I didn't want to do something lame like put another sock on the table, I wriggled and twisted under the table until I had managed to remove my trousers and my shorts. It was a trial to get my trousers back up over what had become a very erect cock, but I managed it and carefully zipped myself back up. Kirsty and Chloe were giggling like schoolgirls as I dropped my shorts on the table with a satisfied grin. And so it went for several more hands with the pile now resembling a load of laundry.

"Last call gentleman…hurry up gentlemen…it's time!"

The pub was closing and the pile of clothing had grown larger at our table. Suddenly Carol was standing beside us with a poorly concealed smirk on her face.

"We're closing up now."

Glancing at the cards and the assorted pile of pants and lingerie, Carol suggested that we take our game and our drinks to my room. We nicked some short stools from a nearby table and started to stumble up the stairs to my room. We piled into one another in a heap of laughter when Kirsty dropped her bra on the floor and stopped in mid-stride to retrieve it. Although the other drinkers in the pub turned for a quick look at the disturbance, British reserve won out and they turned back to their drinks, leaving us alone.

My room had taken on a chill in my absence so I quickly prodded the fire into a bit more action and tossed some chunks of peat on. The radiator, as usual in this country, was cold. Chloe was still wearing her warm jumper, but her sister had been wearing only a thin white blouse against which her now hard nipples pressed enticingly. Both women stood before the fire as the embers began to glow. While the women warmed themselves Simon grudgingly helped me pull the heavy wood table into the middle of the room. I think he fancied the sisters' bodies, but resented them for the status they seemed to have achieved. I didn't really mind because I was having the time of my life.

Finally the room was toasty warm and all of us were perched on the stools around the table with a new hand of cards. Simon's drinking had obviously taken its toll and he was getting even thicker in the head than he had earlier been. He had been winning, but now his luck faded and his clothing came off quickly and joined the rest on the table. I was already down to my shirt, one sock, and my watch. I was acutely aware of my balls resting on the cold, polished wood stool. My cock was comfortably between being flaccid and ready-to-roar, a warm glow really.

"Fuck this," Simon bellowed as he lost yet another hand. He only had his shorts left. He stood up and we expected him to drop them, but instead he tumbled over onto the sofa and more or less passed out. The rest of us looked at each other in surprise and a bit of relief. Kirsty was down to her suspender belt while Chloe was wearing two shoes and a smile. I still had the shirt on my back and a wrist watch. God these women were gorgeous. I had forgotten how beautiful young skin can be and how firm the flesh is. I wondered what it might be like to feast on the feminine flesh around this table.

Chloe's elbows were propped upon the table with her breasts pressed lightly against the table's edge. She was completely unabashed. Her brown nipples had warmed in the room and were no longer fully erect, but ever so slightly raised. Thinking about how the crumpled skin of her aureoles would feel against my tongue teased my cock into lengthening and creeping along the stool until it dropped off the edge.

Chloe folded and rose to remove one shoe. It was then I noticed one more difference between the twins as Chloe's dark hair was neatly trimmed and framed above the lips of her cunt. Kirsty, I had noticed earlier, was untouched and full with a small tattoo near the bones of her hip. I meant to ask her about that later. Kirsty took the hand and I willingly gave up my shirt, having by now lost all inhibition.

A new hand was dealt and I was delighted by the prospects of perhaps actually winning this game and being the one to pose a dare to my fellow players. One card was all I needed and then nobody could beat me. My heart beat in anticipation and I had to remember to even breathe. I was dealt my card, but it wasn't enough. Chloe plopped down three of a kind with a delighted giggle and a devious grin in my direction. I slowly removed my watch and set it on the table. Kirsty looked at Chloe, wondering what she would say next.

Chloe played with me, looking all around the room and at the ceiling before propping her chin on her head, and looking me straight in the eyes. Chloe's hands were trembling slightly. She began to speak with a nervous jitter in her voice.

"Tell me about your ultimate fantasy," she said simply and waited. Kirsty's eyes turned to me. My cock surged beneath the table as Chloe reached down and removed her last shoe, tossing it lightly aside onto the floor.

"Hmmmm," I pretended to mull it over in my mind.

"My fantasy," I slowly started, " would be to find myself in a small room with two beautiful women at my beck and call."

"Every man's fantasy!" laughed Kirsty as I continued.

"I would want to feel them flow over my body like spirits from the moors and worship me like a god until I couldn't resist them any more and needed to possess them."

Kirsty took one look at Simon snoring on the sofa and slinked under the table. In seconds I felt her tiny, cool fingers wrap around my cock, stroking it softly before taking just the tip between her lips. I closed my eyes and felt my mind swirl in disbelief.

Chloe stood slowly and drifted gracefully behind me, pressing her breasts into my back, and softly stroking her hands over my shoulders and chest. Her warm lips pressed lightly to the nape of my neck and began to kiss me. She pulled away and, taking my head in her hands, motioned me to follow her to the massive wood-framed bed in the centre of the room. Kirsty crawled like a cat from beneath the table and up onto the bed. Chloe drew down the thick duvet covering the bed and pressed me down upon my back. I closed my eyes with a sigh as I felt the sisters' light, nimble bodies nestle down on either side of my hips. Two pairs of hands began to gingerly stroke my thighs and tease my cock. Cool palms caressed the warm, tender flesh of my balls. Tiny heads with feathery soft hair rested gently upon my hips as the touches began to centre more and more on my hardening cock. My hips began to thrust ever so slightly to their rhythm.

I gasped as I felt soft lips and a warm mouth flow around the head of my cock. I don't know which woman it was who was slowly, sensually sliding down the length of my cock. I didn't care. The women took turns teasing and swallowing my cock as I gradually lost myself in the decadent pleasure. I had thought of turning to the women, touching them, pleasing them, but as the waves of pleasure swept over me I surrendered to it and floated wherever it might take me.

Gradually, one of the women began to stroke me more urgently, to fuck me deeply within her mouth. I could hear muffled groans and whimpers escaping from around my cock. Uncontrollable spasms of ecstasy began to grip me. I was vaguely aware of one of the twins slithering up alongside of me, taking my head in her hands, and pressing her lips to mine. Her tongue feverishly pressed its way into my mouth as the lips around my cock became frenzied. I could feel my cum welling up from deep within. I abandoned myself as my orgasm enveloped me. Fingers gripped my cock and a warm mouth engulfed me as my cum flowed from my body and mingled in her mouth.

As my orgasm ebbed away, the mouth on my cock continued to tenderly suck me and coax me while the kisses on my lips became tender, nuzzling ones. I opened my eyes. Kirsty was looking at me with a soft smile. She slowly crept down to join her sister and took my cock into her own mouth. Chloe then appeared beside me and silently kissed me deeply. I could taste my cum in her wet mouth. My cock was already responding to Kirsty's persistent stroking and soft, yielding mouth.

Chloe stopped kissing me for a moment.

"I'm feeling a bit moreish," was all she said with a teasing smile before starting to kiss me again. I knew what she meant as I groaned in pleasure and realised I would have a chance to savour the sisters all night long...

"Meeting adjourned," came an abrupt voice from somewhere in the distance.

Annoyed that once again my reverie had been disturbed, I looked around and saw the other members gathering up papers and standing to leave. My glance caught Chloe's as she closed up her journal. She smiled. I smiled.

I didn't wait around but headed out into the blustery cold of the cobbled streets and went straight to the Black Bull, a pub with rooms on the upper floor...

Susan Van Scoyoc

John Isn't Gay!

"I won't believe it. I can't believe it. He isn't gay. He can't be."

Sara was angry. Damned angry as she walked away from the area outside the gym. She looked at John as he moved towards the first workout machine. Abs he certainly had. It was obvious John came here often. His body showed clearly through his workout clothes. His shorts were of those loose cotton type that hung loosely but at the same time seemed to accentuate the curves of his body. If he had been a woman Sara would have said he was seductive. But as a man...she didn't know what to say except he was clearly "well hung." His tee shirt was one of those cut away types which revealed his dark brown nipples and only slightly lighter skin. Sara felt the spasm in her cunt as she felt the wetness starting.

She moved toward the workout machine nearest John and started to stretch out. So many people coming to the gym forgot this essential part of working out and disappeared shortly after because they had torn a muscle shocked into suddenly lifting weights. Sara noticed John glancing over at her as she worked her legs and back. She knew John could see a woman with shapely legs and firm buttocks as he used his own workout machine.

Sara moved to her first machine. Her focus now was on John, the visual impact of her moves, her strength on this man. She could tell he was watching her. Although there were those men who came to the gym almost of a way of life (those who looked as though they ate steroids for breakfast or those who came to pick up women) John fit neither category. Sara had never seen him openly chatting someone up—of either sex. She couldn't believe he was interested in men—he was so good looking. Then she remembered her friend's rueful words one day at a meeting "all the best looking ones are gay."

Sara started to work the first machine. She knew she looked good and worked hard at keeping that way. She moved smoothly with firm movements. Except today. Every so often she spent time lingering over her movements and lingering over her own body. She knew John was watching as she stroked her fingers tenderly over her shoulder and then down over her full breasts. Her nipples, always pert, stood up taller as she caressed herself.

Timing was all important Sara realised as she manipulated it to arrive at the same workout machine at the same time as John. Always the lady Sara offered John first go but instead of moving on to another machine she stood close by taking the chance to talk. First she commented on John's form and then tentatively moved on to how good he looked. He was clearly a virgin as far as pick up lines go. He was hanging on her every word, with his eyes riveted to her nipples! He was clearly shy, saying as little as possible but clearly interested.

Sara took the lead and invited John to the club bar. She wriggled into her tight T shirt after her workout and the slip on skirt—easy and comfortable after a long day. John was there in the bar, as were the two jerks who had started all this. Sara moved over to John and sat close, reaching out to touch John's arm.

"They think you're gay but I know better," Sara whispered, nodding over toward the jerks. "Let's give them a show…" And she lent forward to kiss John full on the lips. Sara reached down and stroked John's thigh, feeling him stir in his seat, unable to believe what was happening to him.

Sara felt John start to respond to her, the pressure of his kiss growing harder, just as the firmness in his groin was growing firmer. Sara stepped closer and with lips still locked guided him to stand and stepped so the length of their bodies touched. Sara could feel the warmth of his body heat and the firmness of those well worked out muscles. She pulled her lips from his and took hold of John's hand to guide him towards the ladies room at the side of the bar. Sara knew they were being watched and didn't care. The desire for this lean muscled body had reached such a pitch inside her that dare or no dare she wanted to fuck him—here—now.

As they walked into the ladies room Sara knew just where to go. There was a wide cubicle for the disabled at the far side of the room. She pulled John after her and locked the door. John looked about to say something when Sara pressed her lips once again over his whilst reaching straight for his cock. Her eyes had been right and what she had seen was now confirmed by her fingers wrapped round his large, almost trembling cock. Sara slipped down the length of John's body and gently released his cock and engulfed it in her wet, swollen lips.

Having just worked out and showered this man tasted so good. Sara had intended to fuck him but—kneeling here as John lent back against the cubicle wall, head thrown back, eyes closed gently moaning—Sara was hooked. She tasted the subtle sweetness of the first drops of pre-cum gathering at the tip of John's cock. Her tongue danced and licked the tip as Sara moved herself so she could take more of him into her deep warm mouth. At the same time she reached her own hand down under her skirt and started firmly stroking her swollen mound. Sara felt her own wetness and pressed harder against her clit whilst firmly taking John into her mouth, sucking harder and harder. She was frenzied as John shuddered, seemed to swell ever bigger inside her and then burst between her teeth filling her mouth with sweet honeyed cum. Sara didn't let go. She held his cock firmly, sucking all of John's juices as she frantically bucked her hips for a few final strokes before she too exploded with a cry forcing her to open her mouth wide. Both were left slumped in the cubicle recovering from the intensity of their respective orgasms.

Then, straightening their clothes, Sara and John walked out into the bar—to a round of applause!

Jason Charles

Job Satisfaction

Mr. Harold G. Wolfe was a fair man. He had a reputation as an old-fashioned, up-standing man with high morals. He was harsh too. Harsh, cold, and, when he needed to be, cruel. Everybody knew this. Most of all though Jennifer Hall and Samuel Colbridge knew this. If you did your job he was good to you. He would look after you. If you did anything that he perceived to be detrimental to the company, the multi-million pound company that he owned and had built from nothing, then he was ruthless. There had never been any second chances for anybody who had crossed him.

Jennifer and Samuel also knew that there was a vacancy in upper management and as always Mr. Wolfe would promote from within. They also knew, as did everyone else in the office, that service was everything in Wolfe's book, and Jennifer and Samuel were holding onto the two longest records. It would be one of them that would be promoted. One of them would, overnight, earn four times as much as the other. One of them would have the opportunity to travel the world on one of the most flattering of expense accounts in the industry. One of them, and only one of them, would have the best insurance, health care, and support that money could buy, because as everyone knew Mr. Wolfe valued his staff above everything else.

There had never been a woman in upper management. This was not because of prejudice on Wolfe's behalf. He had always promoted the best candidate. He was too shrewd to allow petty outdated ideas cloud his decisions. Then again he would not promote Jennifer as some kind of token gesture either. It was quite simple. Jennifer and Samuel had equal lengths of service. Wolfe had his own criteria for selecting the right person for promotion that only he, and the selection committee, was aware of. They were both in with an equal shout just as long as neither of them did anything that he disapproved of in the meantime. It was a two horse race and there could only be one winner.

They were both good looking. Jennifer with her soft short brown hair, her all over tan, shapely figure, and beautifully round bust. And Samuel with his piecing eyes, his strong powerful voice, and his shock of blonde hair. They seemed to be so equal in everything but only one of them would emerge with the great new package that was on offer.

Jennifer and Samuel stopped their conversation for a moment and smiled at Mr. Wolfe as he came back from lunch at The Ritz. In a couple of days time one of them would be joining him. They watched him walk down to the end of the corridor and disappear around the corner on his way to his executive suite. Once he was out of sight Samuel resumed their conversation. "I'd like to say right now Jennifer that I admire your integrity. A lot of women, I'd even go as far as to say most women, would have brought their hem line up if they got even so much as a sniff of a promotion like this one. Not you though, oh no, there it is still just below the knee as it has been for the last five years." He sniggered to himself and looked at her legs under the desk just to confirm what he had said. "And do you know something Jenny, sorry Jennifer, do you know something Jennifer it's the exact reason why you're not going to get the job. A good businessman, that's right I said businessman, would use anything that he could to get what he wanted. Not you though eh? No you're happy to cling to a set of outdated principles and blow your only chance of gaining any kind of advantage over me. Wolfe knows it. He knows that I've got that hunger, that will to succeed, but you—come on why don't you pull out and save yourself the embarrassment?"

Jennifer smiled at him. He was such a smug little shit. What did he mean by "save yourself the embarrassment," she wondered. She knew that there was something in what he was saying. But then on the day that they had given in their applications for the new post Mr. Wolfe had called them into that plush office of his—the one with the breathtaking view of the city from thirty floors up—and told them that any stunts they might try and pull would count for nothing. It was on their past records that he would make his decision just as long as they didn't screw up in the meantime. "Yes well you'd only try and go one better wouldn't you Sam? I couldn't stand the thought of you walking around the office in nothing but a leather g-string, just for Mr. Wolfe's pleasure. If I wanted to get on his good side I'd drop to my knees and go down on him like you've been doing for the past five years," she grinned back at him. "Go and sit back at your own desk Sam. You are disturbing me and I'm running out of patience with you."

"That's okay, I was just leaving for lunch anyway. Of course in forty-eight hours I'll be lunching an hour earlier with the rest of the upper management team."

He shot another grin at her. He had the face of a fashion model and the body of an athlete and he knew it and maybe, more importantly, he knew how to use it. He had fucked just about all of the girls in the office at some time or another and his wife was, as Jenny had once overheard some of the guys in the upper management team describe her, a walking wet dream. There were a lot of advantages to the company if they, that is Mr. Wolfe, picked Sam. He was popular and his wife would be such a hit at all of those in company dinner parties, not to mention her role in wooing the heads of corporations that they did business with. Jenny was not married and wouldn't be in the immediate future either as far as she could see. Mr. Wolfe liked his staff to be married. He'd talked about his wife enough for her to know that.

She wondered why she was doing this to herself. She knew that Sam was only trying to wind her up but he was right. What chance did she really have? Mr. Wolfe had had plenty of opportunities to tell her one way or another, but then she had never broached the subject. She had not wanted to appear mercenary and she hoped that Mr. Wolfe understood that. But then how could he know how much she wanted this promotion if she had never told him.

Jenny threw her pen down. What was the use she asked herself? It was time for her lunch too. Maybe she should buy a shorter skirt—not that it would make any difference to her application—but it might just unnerve Sam. She considered this as she picked up her coat and made for her favourite coffee shop.

Sam was actually skipping lunch today as well as a date with that new hot little bitch secretary from accounts with the big bimbo eyes and the stand up and suck me tits. Instead he was making his way across the city to a photography studio run by one of his old school friends. If the pictures came out right, as he wanted them to, then he would soon be sitting in the lap of luxury in an office like Wolfe's with a full view of the city below and the comings and goings of the vermin they called the workers.

He had dreamt about this moment. Now he could almost smell it all, the Champagne and Caviar, the fresh leather seats of the Jag he would ask for, the sweet perfume of the air hostesses in the first class section of the plane, and the musk of the impressed beautiful women who would be more than happy to open their legs for someone earning so much money. He was not going to let prissy Jennifer Hall fuck it up for him. And so he had waited and waited and then about two weeks ago his opportunity finally fell into his lap.

He had been friends with the security guard Bill Houston for quite a while. Occasionally he'd drop by to say hello, either morning, lunchtime, or when he was leaving at the end of the day. It depended on which shift Bill was on. Two weeks ago Bill showed him something very interesting, a video recording from one of the office CCTV cameras. He had not recognised her at first. It was obviously a woman getting changed but the lights were dim and it was difficult to make anything out. It seemed like a laugh, a little bit of homemade pornography of the kind that he was partial to himself. Then she stepped into the light for a moment. She was a fantastic looking specimen Bill had said and he was right. She was wearing a see-through black dress that finished at the top of her thighs. Underneath her pert firm breasts were held in the skimpiest of black bras and the tiniest of tight black panties covered her crotch. She stooped to zip up a pair of black knee high Cuban heeled boots that all the teenagers seemed to be wearing at the moment and then she finished this all off with a slim black mask decorated with sequins which covered her nose and eyes.

Sam and Bill watched open-mouthed as she walked away from the camera down the corridor. "Can we follow her on another camera?" he had asked Bill. It was no problem and now they switched to a shot of the hall and watched her long legs and perfectly formed ass move elegantly as she made her long strides. They then watched her take a key out from under the elastic of those panties. Sam thought, as she reached down, that she was going to take them off and could feel his cock throbbing in his trousers. She took out the key though and opened one of the upper management office doors.

As she disappeared behind the door Bill turned to him. "She's something isn't she? What I'd like to do to a woman like that. Yes she really is something special." Sam had an idea. "Rewind, right back to the beginning. No stop it on the bit with the mask maybe we can freeze it, get a look at her face." Sam did not recognise that figure and he had bagged just about every woman of note in the office at some time or another. He was getting excited maybe; just maybe, it was her, his rival Jenny. The video recording on second, third and fourth viewing confirmed his suspicions. It was perfect. Fate had finally shone on him.

A quick discussion with Bill and a glance at other recordings showed him that she was careful. The first little bit of footage was the best they had got. He needed better evidence if he was going to take it to Wolfe and the partners in upper management. If the evidence wasn't indisputable it might look as if he were purposely trying to blacken her name, which of course he was, but Wolfe didn't take kindly to in house fighting.

A few beers with Bill and he soon got the tip off on where he could get hold of clandestine movement activated cameras and a voice-activated tape recorder. All he had to do was set them up in the office and wait. The next day he took in a whole series of ornaments all with built in lenses that would take great pictures in the dark. Two nights ago Bill had spotted her again. Off she went again in that black sequined mask, those long black boots and a kind of tight black mesh body suit with nothing underneath. Only she was more careful and stayed out of the light and the focus of the camera. Her identity was still inconclusive. Her presence though would have set off the cameras and the tape recorder. The pictures should be ready today. The tape recording he had already listened to. There were two voices one male, one female, and they were distant coming from the other end of the corridor:

Man's voice: "Goddess Gaia holder of the magic of the earth and everything on it how may I serve you tonight? Please inform me of my task. Your beauty blinds me and your power in this realm makes me nothing by comparison. Instruct me so that I may worship you with my service."

Woman's voice: "Get on your knees man. You must be taught to show respect. No man may address this Goddess without first bowing his head."

Man's voice: "Forgive me Goddess Gaia. I beseech you to show mercy."

Woman's voice: "Forgive you! Why should I? It is not for you to ask of me. You must earn forgiveness. Remain on your knees and when I approach you show me your apology with that lusty tongue, put it where I like it to go. And then afterwards if you beg I may consider forgiving you, but then again probably I won't."

It was pretty serious stuff. She was using the offices to turn a few tricks, make a little extra on the side. Sam didn't blame her. The money they were on just wasn't enough, but Wolfe would not tolerate prostitution, especially not on the company premises. She was shafted. Sam laughed it his little joke. He was going to be doing a lot more laughing. He'd got her now just as long as the photographs had caught her. The tape was a good back up, but the voices weren't clear enough and most of the conversation was inaudible. All that he needed was one good face shot and he had her right where he wanted her.

Jenny put down the bag from the boutique where she had just bought that skirt that Sam had suggested to her. It was pale indigo satin and finished above the knee. She had a great pair of high heels to go with it. She crossed her shapely tanned legs as the charming Benito brought over her favourite espresso choc. She stirred in a spoonful of sugar and regarded the handsome Benito for a moment. He was dark and brutal looking but with a warm smile and hairy bullish chest that seemed to pop out from whatever he was wearing. She knew that he had his eye on her and had for some time. She liked the attention and crossed her legs over in the other direction whilst pretending to read the paper. Benito almost jumped out of his pants. She smiled and sipped her coffee.

A group of young girls came in all fawning over him. They called him over to their table and made lewd suggestive comments to him. He joined in their banter—after all it was good for business. The girls obviously appreciated him and made remarks about his bum as he walked back to get their order. Jenny could tell though that he was keeping one eye on her.

He took the girls order over, two cappuccinos, an espresso, and a herbal tea, and then he stopped by her table with a small delicate looking pastry topped with fresh cream cinnamon. "Please for you, with the house."

"You mean on the house," she smiled.

"If you like on the house!"

"Thank you Benito," she rolled his name on her tongue and gently parted her lips placing a small thumb nail size piece in her mouth. "Oh it's exquisite."

"Is a gift for being good customer. If you like maybe you order next time." He leaned over to her closer than usual and then closer still. She could feel her heart beating faster and faster in her chest. "I'm glad you like." She did like and she liked the feeling of all this attention. She saw the look in his eyes, the want, and she imagined his brown hands running up and down her legs, across her bare back, and the hairs on her sweet mound being parted by his long cool fingers.

"Anytime for you," he smiled, waking her from her daydream, his tone suggesting that he was referring to the images in her head rather than the pastry. She too watched his bum as he went back behind the serving bar before going back to pretending read the paper.

He had it. It was perfect. He had almost hugged his old schoolmate but instead invited him to lunch at The Ritz in a week or twos time. It was almost too good to be true.

Sam checked the pictures again when he got back to work. There had been about sixty shots in all, two thirds of which were useless. Of the remaining twenty about half did not include a facial shot. There were nine that were okay-ish but there were three in particular that were just perfect.

One of them showed her in her underwear with the black mesh body suit in her one hand while her other hand was about to remove her sensible but comfortable work panties. It was a three-quarter shot that was unmistakably Jenny. The second shot showed her applying lipstick in a small round personal mirror. Her eyes were wide and her lips puckered. But the third was the icing on the cake. She was sitting at her own desk this time, something that the CCTV camera had missed. Jenny's feet were up on the desk, those high Cuban heels of her boots resting precariously, inches from the edge. The body suit was unfastened at the crotch and there was a silhouette of a man between her thighs tasting her nectar. Jenny's head was thrown back in ecstasy, her short delightful brown hair imperfectly ruffled. She was holding a long cone shaped joint and had obviously just puffed out a great cloud of smoke. Her breasts were shaded seductively by the tight black mesh. Wolfe would hit the roof and Sam knew it. Drugs, even grass, were a big no no to a stern moralist like him. Not only would she not get the promotion but also she would probably, no definitely, get the sack.

Samuel considered this as he looked at this photograph, A4 size in black and white, the enjoyment of cunnilingus etched on her features. He sat alone in the locked cubicle admiring her stunning good looks and that taut looking supple body. Another thought came to him as he unzipped his fly and took out his heavy fat cock and began to stroke it up and down while concentrating on that beautiful photograph. He had plans for Miss Goddess Gaia. He rubbed himself up and down his entire length and imagined her curvaceous legs wrapped around his body, her hot breath on his shoulder, while he put himself hard and sharp into that most desirable of all soft places. He began to rub himself harder as he imagined walking into the office right now and throwing her across her desk, lifting her skirt up, and hammering his stiff cock into her cunt. How she would plead for more, give herself up to him; beg him to be more forceful with each stroke of his length. He dropped the photo to the floor as he clenched his eyes shut and imagined the look of sheer pleasure on her face as he shot his desire into her body. The closed eyes, the open mouth, and the fast heavy inviting breathing that he imagined her to present to all her lovers sent him over the edge, and he ejaculated his victory into the air. The thin white streamers of come were celebrations of the homage that would be paid to him for this master plan.

Jenny checked her e-mail when she got back from flirting with Benito. She ran her well-manicured nails through her short brown hair and moved the mouse impatiently. The thought of Benito had aroused her and the last thing that she wanted was to spend the rest of the afternoon and early evening in the stuffy office. Worse luck there was an e-mail from Sam, no doubt another juvenile attempt at winding her up.

She clicked for the message to come up.

Dear Goddess Gaia of the earth and everything that stands upon it

I thought that you'd appreciate me showing you the picture below before I send a copy to the upper management team. You've really blown it this time. It's a really great picture. You ought to try your hand with magazine photo shoots, the up-market ones of course. All of which begs the question how much do you charge? How much did you charge that guy? Not as though I'm going to be paying you understand. I just thought it'd be nice to tell Wolfe and the rest of the selection committee whether they've got a high-class hooker on the pay roll or just some common slut.

I'm playing squash after work tonight at the company's sports centre. My opponent doesn't like to hang around after so why don't you join me for a drink? Don't worry I'll be upstairs in the bar that sells alcohol (I thought that you'd need a drink) none of those health freaks go in there so we'll have the chance to discuss the situation alone. Look forward to seeing you. Love Samuel

P.S. Do you realise that I'm only one button away from circulating a copy of this picture to everyone in the firm? Well you do now.

He had scanned the photograph in. She had no idea how he could have taken the picture. It was certainly a beautiful picture of her. In fact in different circumstances she would have been quite proud of it, her total beauty and her abandonment of everything but the moment was more than artistic, it was erotic. She was in big trouble though, and she knew it, this could be, would be, the end of her, let alone her chances for promotion. If this got out...

Jenny looked over at Sam's desk he was grinning from ear to ear. She picked up her bag and left the office not looking behind and not saying a word to anyone. "I'll see you tonight," she heard the scumbag whisper as she walked past him. She could still hear laughing as she entered the elevator.

Jenny ordered an ice cold Gin and Tonic and went to sit out of view of the barman in a small secluded booth. Sam was right—there was nobody else in there. The barman had been watching TV when she ordered and looked surprised to have a customer.

She had put on her new skirt that shimmied in the light and set off her heels just as she knew it would. She wore a soft tight white sweater that clung to her chest shaping her eye-catching breasts. Jenny knew that she was going to have to use all of her assets tonight. She would not bow down to Sam, not until she had no choice. She would not give him the satisfaction of her giving in to the little shit. She pulled up her skirt to adjust the top of her pure white stockings and re-clip the suspender. The deeply tanned exposed flesh between her stockings and white lace panties contrasted seductively with the brilliant whiteness of her luxuriant lingerie. The barman brought over her drink and the salacious look on his face told her that he got a glimpse of something that he shouldn't have. He was very polite though and put her drink down and told her to call him over if she wanted anything else. As he walked off he turned to catch her eye and smile again. He was quite cute and in other circumstances she would be tempted to pick him up and take him home for the evening—strictly for one night of course.

After half an hour, another two G and T's and many longer and longer glances from the enthusiastic barman, Sam finally made his entrance. He was all square jawed and freshly showered after his game. He sat down and ordered a Screwdriver. His body gave off a certain coolness after his shower which refreshed her own warm skin. "Did you win?"

"Don't I always?" He was feeling pleased with himself.

"So what did you want to see me about?" She was trying to stay calm and in control but he saw straight through her façade.

"Stop pissing around here Jenny baby. You've fucked up. I mean really fucked up and you know it. Now I was going to ask you to drop out of the race for promotion and we'd forget all about this. I'd destroy the negatives and that would be that. As you know I'm not one to bear a grudge, not usually anyway. But then I got to thinking about things. All of those sexy needy women that I've had in the office, how happy they all were to share something intimate—all of them that is except for you. You've always rejected my advances. You've always thought you were too good for me. Well that's all about to change. Wolfe's always telling me that he won't tolerate drugs, not in his workforce, and you, you like a little smoke don't you? It's okay you don't have to answer me. Understand I quite like a joint myself from time to time, not generally in the position that you like to, but it doesn't bother me. We all have our whims, our fantasies. I don't want to stop anybody living out their dreams you see. You can't say the same though can you?"

"What do you mean?"

"I'm talking about you Jenny. You haven't been bothered to help me with my little fantasy of you. The one where we're in the elevator and I slide my hand up your skirt and finger that moist pussy of yours."

"Oh Sam I never knew..."

"Don't give me that."

Sam stood up and sat next to her. He leaned across her and began to play with her nipple through her soft woolen sweater. Jenny breathed in, sharply shocked by his fast approach. He made a circle with his fingertip and then gently pinched her now stiff nipple until she closed her eyes and showed him her pleasure in a deep breathless sigh. She uncrossed her legs and took her foot and moved it up onto the leather booth seat so that he could see right up her shimmering skirt. "Nice, stockings and suspenders, all in white too, how symbolic. They're expensive too if I'm not mistaken. Then I suppose someone in your profession must have the best. And with your moonlighting you can afford it no doubt." He continued to play with her nipple and began to lightly kiss and bite her neck.

"Only the best for you Sam. I want you to have the best."

The sensations in her nipple and neck were sending shivers of hot and cold throughout her body. Sam dipped his finger in the ice cold gin and ran it up and down her stockinged legs, onto the exposed flesh and then, after teasing her along the elastic, after pretending to push through the white lace, he finally slipped his finger inside her panties and stroked his cold finger up and down the outside of her vagina. He stroked the lips firmly and she could feel his teeth on her neck biting a little harder now. Both of them were breathing fast and heavy.

"I always knew that you would be good Sam. I always knew that you could enjoy a woman. Now take me Sam, come on, hold me open, pin me down, please Sam, open me up until it hurts and then force yourself into me. Now Sam, please for God's sake now!"

Sam was shaking with anticipation. He held her legs in a tight grip and forced them apart while she pretended to resist. To his excitement she began to call out "No Sam, No" really loud so that anyone could hear. It was turning him on more than anybody had ever before. He had to have her and…

He was totally focused now, lost in his lust, unaware of everything but her. He actually got turned on by her calling out, so engrossed in his pleasure, in her fine body that he forgot where he was. Her calls, she was now sure, would bring the barman running to the damsel's rescue. She smiled, men were wonderfully predictable. She could hear the barman now as she called out again "Stop Sam, no, oh God no." The tears that she was concentrating on forming in her eyes would seal his fate.

Then suddenly just as Sam was about to take himself out he stopped. A fierce anger came into his eyes. "I'm not as stupid to do it here, in a public place, not like you. I'm sorry Jenny darling, good try but we're not all as foolish as you are. You won't catch me like that, and you've just made things ten times worse for yourself." Before the barman could see what was happening Sam had stood up. "It's okay we're just leaving, aren't we Jennifer?" He growled through clenched teeth. "Nothing to worry about just a difference of opinion wasn't it sweetie?"

"Are you okay miss?"

She nodded, "Yes everything's fine." The barman didn't believe her and she appreciated him for it but he would do nothing and all three of them knew it.

"Like I said," Sam growled again, "we're just leaving." He grabbed Jenny's wrist and dragged her out of the bar.

They went down many flights of stairs. Sam was still holding onto her tightly. "Where are we going?"

"Somewhere where we won't be disturbed, where you can't scheme against me you hot little bitch." He took her down to the underground car park. Sam had a very nice new shiny blue BMW. He pressed the button on his key ring to unlock the doors and told her to get in. "Where are we going?" she demanded as she fastened her seatbelt.

"Nowhere!" and at that he released her seatbelt and hastily reclined her seat so that she was thrown backwards. He scrambled on top of her pushing his hands up her sweater, grasping her flesh, and squeezing her breasts together. He used his strength to open her legs wide apart so that her skirt rode up and he quickly snatched her panties down.

Jenny could feel his whole weight upon her. He moved frantically trying to make her submit to him. She was no slouch and could have fought him off only—somewhere in the back of her mind—she realised that she had always wanted this, not Sam, but this, this wild need for her. Her sweater was half off, above her head, but binding her arms together. It was good to be the helpless one for once. She rested her feet upon the dashboard as Sam pulled her bra around her waist and began nibbling on her tits. She could feel every movement of his tongue and the harsh but exhilarating grip of his hands.

Maybe I should throw him off now, she thought as he began to push two fingers in and out of her wet cunt. But it felt so good to her, an unexpected thrill that was all the more exciting because she should have stopped him. He was good though, too good to resist for any longer and she began to push her pelvis up so that his fingers would get deeper into her. She rubbed her knee between his legs and felt the stiff reassurance of him. He fumbled to free himself obviously enjoying the feeling of her leg against him.

Then he was free. He quickly held her down so that she couldn't move, or at least pretended that she couldn't, and thrust himself up into her. It was good. She cried out in pleasure and pain impaled on his cock and wanting more. His free hands now smoothed over her pulsing clit. She had surrendered to his total control now. She thrust back with each bang of his cock into her cunt and each new push on her shining pink clitoris. Her body began to tighten and spasm in the glory of this wonderful fuck when Sam threw her onto the back seat.

He manhandled her onto all fours and then stroked her vagina from behind. She heard a not unfamiliar buzzing sound and turned to see a large vibrator going off in his hand that he'd obviously taken from the now open glove compartment. The noise itself always turned her on. She had one just like it at home only in blue not purple. It was one of her better ones and she couldn't wait to be teased with it. Only Sam didn't tease her. He stuck it straight up her juicy hole and turned it up to maximum. He held it there for a while and then let it rest against the leather seat so that she could slide up and down on it. He reached round with another hand and moved his fingers quickly over her needy clit. He squeezed her tits mercilessly with his other hand.

Then suddenly her whole body began to move in waves of pure joy as if a hot pleasurable electric shock was passing through her as he pressed his whole hard shaft up her arse. He fucked her hard and she moved on the vibrator and he rubbed her clit in what seemed like all directions at once. Then she felt it begin inside her. The feeling was overwhelming and she encouraged it. Jenny was going to orgasm on the back seat of his car and as she closed her eyes it felt as if she was being fucked by two guys and she was enjoying the work of two hard men inside her and that thought went from her mind right down to her toes and back again. And she could tell that her increased arousal was having its effect on

Sam because he was bigger than ever now and he was fucking her faster and harder than she had ever known.

Then, with their bodies writhing together they came in what seemed like a fountain of lust and sex. They collapsed onto the back seat together both of them relaxing into their satisfaction. Jenny could feel that the inside of her quim was still contracting.

"This doesn't change a thing you know Jenny. You're good, real good, so good in fact that you won't be needing your job anymore, with that kind of action you'll probably make more than me."

"What makes you so sure that I'm for sale?"

"Come off it. Anyway I was going to let you keep your job but now I don't think it's such a good idea. I'd have to constantly look over my shoulder. I know you Jenny you wouldn't rest until you got revenge."

"You bastard Sam. I don't think you've got the nerve to show Wolfe those pictures. I'll say it's a set up that you forced yourself on me just because I refused you."

"Yeah go ahead, who'll believe you? Nobody's going to believe a slut from the street over me now are they."

"What about the barman he knew something was going on? He'd side with me."

"Oh get real, you just virtually raped me if you remember?"

"I'm going to fucking kick the shit out of you," Jenny said as she went to punch him with her strongest fist. Sam avoided the blow though, which would have broken his nose if it had hit its intended target. He opened the door behind her and kicked her out onto the concrete floor of the car park. He started the engine up.

"You fucking coward!" she screamed. "Come back and fight!"

The electric window came down and he threw her panties out at her and laughed, "Well that's easy for you to say. See you bright and early tomorrow morning and don't be late—not for your last day at work."

Sam sped off, leaving Jenny to pick herself up, dust herself off, and make the long journey home.

The next morning Jennifer forlornly made her way to the office. She was ready though. She knew that all was not lost—not yet. She put on a sharp blue pinstriped trouser suit and the highest heels she could walk in. She wanted to look intimidating. She wanted to appear confident, and she would. She pulled a face at that shit Sam as she passed his desk. There was one day until Wolfe made his decision. Would Sam show him the pictures? Would she miss out on promotion? The answers, she knew, to both questions would be yes. Maybe he wouldn't freak out, but then she expected that he would. Maybe he'd let her keep her job, at least until she found another one, then again most probably he wouldn't. There was nothing left to do but give it her best shot, one last show for posterity.

Sam stood up picked up the A4 sized envelope and held it securely to his chest. Jenny smiled, as if she'd try anything as juvenile as to try and steal his precious pictures. He was gone maybe fifteen minutes before she got a call from Wolfe's personal assistant instructing her to go to his office immediately. She stood up to her full height which was quite something in her highest heels and set off for Mr. Wolfe's office.

As she entered, Mr. Wolfe and Samuel were just finishing their conversation.

"I thank you for your diligence Sam. Your work will not go unnoticed. We need more men of your calibre on the team."

Jenny had been unsure of how to approach Mr. Wolfe about this but now she was in here, and after hearing the same old backslapping tone, that we're all men together bullshit, in Mr. Wolfe's praise of Sam, she was sure. Sam winked cockily at her as he left. He was so sure of himself that he hadn't listened to her.

Jennifer sat down as Mr. Wolfe's gesture invited. The great desk that was a symbol of his power was just in front of the huge windows that looked down on the city. Only the blinds were drawn as it was so early and the boss had not had time to open them. It was time to put her plan into action.

"Do you mind if I just open the blinds and let some daylight in Mr. Wolfe?" She had stood up and walked over to the blinds before he could answer. "That's better now isn't it Mr. Wolfe? Or should I say Mr. Big Bad Wolfe?" She moved swiftly over to his desk, opened the bottom drawer on the left-hand side and took out the handcuffs which she quickly fastened around his wrists, pulling them hard behind his back. "And haven't I told you to stand up when your Goddess enters the room?" She stepped up onto his desk and stood before him. "Well?"

"Yes Goddess Gaia, always Goddess Gaia."

"Well stand then!" she admonished.

Goddess Gaia unfastened her trousers and let them slip down her smooth legs to her feet. She stepped out of them and reaching down to the sharp blade of one of his letter openers. He backed away but nearly overbalanced, obviously uncomfortable with his hands locked in the shiny metal cuffs. Jenny moved to the edge of the desk. She brandished the letter opener before him and with two sharp movements cut away her silky black knickers showing her neat mound of black hair.

"You've been careless you weak pathetic little man. We've been watched. You must think up a suitable punishment for this insolent wretched Samuel while I think up a suitable punishment for you."

Mr. Wolfe trembled with excitement. "Of course, whatever pleases you my Goddess."

"That's right whatever pleases me. In the meantime I'm going to stand and look down at my world, survey my earth, and you are going to begin your worship. And when I've soaked up everything you've got to offer I'm going to discard you, throw you aside and make you watch as another hundred worshipers take your place." At that she spitefully grabbed his hair and thrust his face between her legs where his tongue began to probe within her.

Soon it would be flicking across her clit at what would seem like a million miles an hour. She would feel its warm wetness within her, on her thighs, on her clit, in her mind. And she would come with his face nestled between her legs and then she would come again and again as often as she liked while she decided exactly which important position of power she would accept tomorrow.

Stephen Van Scoyoc
The Seduction

I first saw her at a party friends of mine were hosting. It was a pretty lame party—not because my friends were lame—but because most of those attending were lame. They were middle-aged and it showed. They were proud of it. The men were dull and talked only of business or football, trying to outdo one another on either the bank account or the football pitch or both. The women too were mostly dull, like the English weather. Most wore frumpy, loose fitting clothes of black, grey, or, worse yet, flowers. Their hair was cut short and they wore the expressions of women who had sucked lemons for a lifetime. Their chatter was dominated by kids, private schools, and summer holidays in Spain.

One woman was stunningly different from the rest. I had never seen her before, but she was moving our way with a glass of white wine. I guessed she was about thirty with long raven hair, dark eyes that flashed fire, and a slender body barely concealed beneath a "little black number". I was sitting on the floor, the only man in the company of a handful of the more interesting women attending the party. We had been discussing literature and, as usual, when it got out that I was an author and lecturer a small group quickly formed up to chat about books. I have to admit, I've always enjoyed the attention being an author gives me. The woman held back just at the edge of the circle, eavesdropping on our conversation.

Jackie, who had been sitting beside me eagerly chattering away, invited her to join us and introduced her to me as Marie. I rose to my knees as she leant down and gently shook her hand. Gracefully, Marie folded her legs up and sat down on the floor in our little group. I couldn't help but notice the way she held her glass with a delicacy and sensual grace. Her fingers were long and slender with manicured nails and a European flavour. She slipped into the conversation as easily as she had settled onto the floor. Her long hair flowed over her shoulders onto her back and over her breasts. The black dress she wore caressed her body like the gentlest of hands and responded to her every movement. When her glass was empty I watched as her fingers absentmindedly traced lines over the cool globe and rounded edge of the crystal. There was a sensual quality lurking just beyond reach—a sensuality I was drawn to.

Marie had arrived late at the party—and alone. Her husband had promised to attend with her but, as usual, rang up at the last moment to say he was grabbing a drink in London with his colleagues. Marie knew that this meant he would stumble in late, waking her, and wanting a quick fuck before he quickly dropped off to sleep. She would do her duty—of course—and then masturbate furiously, half out of anger and half out of unfulfilled frustration while he snored beside her.

I excused myself for a moment, taking Marie's empty wine glass, and returned in a few moments with full glasses. As I handed Marie's glass to her I felt her fingers softly slip over mine like a warm breath before lifting the glass away from my hand. Her eyes met mine and a subtle smile flickered across her face. I felt even more drawn to her than ever. I had momentarily thought of seducing her, but now I wasn't sure who was doing the seducing and I'm even less sure if she was aware of the animal magnetism she exuded.

The rest of the group had disbanded during my brief departure—perhaps sensing the electricity in the air—leaving me in the intimate company of Marie. Marie was English, but of European descent blending Spanish and French blood. It explained her dark hair, dark eyes, and brown skin—such a contrast to the pale ivory pallor of the English—and the lovely lilt to her voice. The wine quickly evaporated, loosening our restraint. Marie mentioned that she had just watched *Bridges of*

Madison County on BBC the week before. She said it with a certain reserve as though waiting for me to dismiss it with disinterest—a chick flick. Rather, I enthusiastically offered that it was one of the most erotic films I had ever seen.

"I know just how she felt when Robert left," she said with longing in her voice. "I kept saying 'open the door—open the damn door and just go with him'"

I could see her eyes misting over as she thought about it and realised that Marie was feeling the things many women her age do. The romance and adventure is gone long before a woman is starting to feel her most sensuous. She grew silent and looked down at her empty glass, watching her fingertips draw slowly over the lip. Then she looked up brightly at me and spoke.

"You know the part where her kids are reading her letters? When they call her Anaïs Nin?"

I nodded.

"Well, I went to the book shop and found a second-hand edition of one of her books. It's called *A Literate Passion* I think."

I knew the book she meant—have a well-read copy of it myself.

"God—to have such passion for someone must be incredible!"

Marie had become completely relaxed and animated as we talked about juicy bits in the book and about whether Anaïs had kept her husband Hugh completely in the dark about her escapades with Henry Miller. We talked for more than an hour—until the party was starting to break up. We both stood up, aware that our growing intimacy might attract some unwanted attention. She held her hand out to me and, as we clasped, told me I really must come around for tea so we could talk some more. I told her I would love to and gave her one of my cards. We kissed each other on the cheeks—have to love those European customs—and I felt a tingling shock as her breasts pressed softly to my chest. The look in her eyes told me she had felt it too.

A week or two passed and I had all but given up on hearing from Marie again. I didn't even know her surname so I couldn't ring her and I wasn't about to ask the party's host for her name. Then, as I checked my email one morning, there was a short message from her. It read simply, "Tea today…11.00? Just show up…Marie." Her address was at the bottom. I decided I wasn't going to miss this chance.

Marie's house was in a posh area and reflected the success of her husband's work in London. I knocked on the door and Marie was instantly there, ushering me in. She looked fabulous with her long dark hair glistening and bounding down in loose locks about her shoulders. She kissed my cheeks in greeting as the door closed behind us. Marie had been sitting by a small table beside a large window framing the back garden. Brightly coloured leaves drifted in the breeze on the swimming pool as the low autumn sun beamed. I noticed that Anaïs Nin's *Delta of Venus* was turned face down on the table. It certainly gave us something to talk about.

I sat down at the table while Marie fetched the tea and cups from the kitchen. I could hear the kettle starting to boil and clink of expensive china as it was set on the tray. I looked around at the house. It was immaculate—considering that Marie had two school-age children—and perfect in every way. I stole a glance at the book. She was reading "The Basque and Bijou". I heard her returning and quickly put the book back.

Marie began to pour the tea when I said simply "The Basque and Bijou huh?"

Marie quivered a bit, nearly spilling the tea, and blushed. Her blush quickly faded as she sat down opposite me and moved the book aside.

"I thought I was the only one who felt this way. Anaïs writes about things I've felt and she's done the things I long to do."

Marie continued.

"I showed the book to my husband. He flipped through it and said 'where's the pictures' and then tossed it back to me saying it looked boring."

Marie sighed.

I told Marie about the movie that had been made of the book—that it was so delicious and erotic that she must find a copy of it somewhere. We talked for an hour or more, finishing our pot of tea. The school bell rang in the distance and the children's voices disappeared as they returned to classes from the playground. Marie looked up and out the window. It was only 1.00 PM and already the sun was dipping low again.

"I'll get us some more tea," Marie offered as she stood up and walked toward the kitchen. I decided to follow her a few seconds later.

When I entered the kitchen, Marie was facing the cupboards. I'm sure she heard me walking up, but she didn't turn. I studied her. Marie was wearing a baggy burgundy jumper over tight fitting, black jeans. I recalled what Marie had looked like in that black dress at the party and thought what a shame it was to hide herself in that jumper.

I padded softly up directly behind her and softly rested my hands on her shoulders before brushing them down along her back. Her response was unmistakable. Marie's neck arched back and a sigh escaped from her lips. I let my hands rest gently in the hollow of her narrow waist as I stepped up close enough to press my body ever so slightly to hers. The fragrance of her hair filled my nose as my lips tenderly planted a kiss on the bare skin of her neck. Marie released herself and nuzzled back into my body. We stood like that for quite a long time before I turned her around the face me.

I looked into Marie's face. Her eyes were so dark and deep—accentuated by carefully applied makeup to give a sultry air to her gaze. She looked briefly into my eyes and then looked down toward my chest. I raised my fingers to her face, to stroke the downy soft hairs on her neck, below her ears. The cool silver of her hoop earrings brushed tantalizingly against the backs of my hands. Marie's eyes closed and she took in a deep breath. I continued to stroke her softly beneath her ears, marvelling at her response, as she pressed her soft body closer and closer into mine. I could feel my own arousal building, knew that she could feel my hard cock pressing into her, wanting her. Marie's hands clinched tightly onto my shirt as her breathing began to come in short, quiet gasps. Then I felt Marie tense and shudder and almost fall into me. I was surprised to think that a woman could have an orgasm simply from being close to a lover who stroked her face.

"God," she gasped softly, "that was wonderful."

I agreed. I pressed my lips toward her and she met me in a slow, deep, sensual kiss. Our bodies were pressed tightly together, both of us beginning to grind our hips against the other with a hunger that neither of us was going to deny. By now our arms were wrapped tightly around one another. Her body was even slimmer than I had imagined beneath that bulky jumper and the sensation of her full, soft breasts against my chest was exquisite. I allowed my hands to slip beneath her jumper to stroke against her smooth skin. As my hands flowed higher up her body Marie stepped back slightly and in one deft motion lifted the jumper from her body. Her beauty was breathtaking.

Marie's dark brown skin was smooth and her flesh toned. Her skin was in delicious contrast to the lacy, almost sheer Gossard bra she was wearing. I think she had dressed just for this. Her nipples were the darkest of brown and pressed hard against the tight fabric. My cock was so hard that it ached against my now tight trousers. Marie's hand brushed over the obvious bulge before pulling me tightly against her again.

"Let's go in the lounge," she urged as she pulled away and led me toward a massive leather sofa. Marie kicked off her shoes as we walked and turned to face me upon reaching the sofa. Marie unbuttoned her trousers and stepped out of them. I was so taken by her that I nearly forgot to start taking off my own clothes. It was odd, there was none of this shyness one might expect between two new lovers. Just an instant acceptance and ferocious desire. I looked at her body and she looked at mine. Her body was slender and fit. Marie's breasts were the same tone of brown as the rest of her skin with large brown nipples and the firmness of a much younger woman. Her body slimmed to a tight waist before flaring out again into the slim hips of a European woman. I wanted her then. I wanted her there.

In a flash we were both naked and pressing our flesh together. None of the furtive groping of teenagers secluded in the back of a car. Marie laid down upon the buttery soft Italian leather and parted her legs to me. I think she expected me to immediately climb upon her and enter her, but I stopped short because I wanted to taste her and feel the lush softness of her cunt against my lips. I wanted to feel her wetness against my skin. I kissed the insides of her thighs tenderly and welcomed the moans of pleasure she answered with. Gently I stroked my tongue over her lips, barely touching her, and inhaling the musky aroma that drove me on mindlessly. My hands began to stroke her waist and tummy as I pressed my tongue more deeply into Marie. She was so wet and tasted so wonderful that I couldn't bear to leave just yet.

Marie began to undulate her hips slowly and I carefully matched her rhythm, wanting to feel her release, urging her on until she relented. I could sense her balancing on the edge, teetering on the brink, as her moans became more insistent. I drew my hand over her thigh and began to press a single finger into her cunt. Slowly, luxuriously I felt the snug warmth of her body swallowing my finger as I continued to stroke with my tongue. Before my finger was very deep Marie sucked in a deep breath and bolted almost upright, shuddering violently. I held still as I felt her cunt tightening on my finger. Her hands gripped my head and held it as though in a vice. Gradually her body softened and relaxed back into the creamy leather, her gorgeous hair splayed out around her head like a pool of black water.

As she relaxed, Marie's body opened up to me and I crawled up between her legs. Lifting her legs slightly I began to draw the length of my cock between the swollen lips of her cunt. Each time the head of my cock bobbed over her clit she would gasp and cry out. Finally, I could resist her no longer. I pressed the head of my cock just inside of her, feeling her tightness, feeling the delicious warmth flowing over my cock as I slowly slipped deeper and deeper. I was dizzy and delirious with pleasure. I felt as though my entire body was being swallowed up by Marie, filling her. We began to move slowly together, savouring the sensations as my cock glided within her cunt. Sometimes stroking in and out with decadent slowness and at other times moving together with my cock filling her as deeply as possible. Our ecstasy continued to climb with abandon.

Marie's breath came in ragged gasps as she began to thrust hungrily toward me. I felt my cock swell in anticipation with each thrust of her body. I wanted to bury myself deep within her. I wanted to fill her with my cum. I wanted to hear her scream in ecstasy. Her gasps became sharp cries. Her sharp cries became hoarse screams. Then with one final, agonising thrust Marie again bolted up against my body, bucking in the tide of orgasm as it swept over her, consumed her, and gripping me tightly with inhuman strength. Marie flung her head back against the sofa and let loose a scream as my own orgasm overtook me and the warmth of my cum flowed between us. I collapsed on top of Marie.

After a few moments, afraid that my weight might crush her I started to shift slightly, but Marie grabbed me suddenly, pulled me tight, and said "Don't even fucking move!" I didn't have to be told twice! My cock was still hard and as we lay silently, unmoving, I could feel her pulse squeezing my cock and every little twinge of my cock made Marie whimper. I was surprised to feel my cock getting even harder, rather than softer. I was completely lost in the sensation when Marie started to wriggle out from beneath me. As my cock pulled free of her our mingled cum flooded out onto her husband's favourite leather sofa. Marie seemed unconcerned.

Marie gently pushed me onto my back, parted my legs, and nestled down between them. By now my cock, glistening and wet, was standing up hard and straight. She wrapped her hand around it firmly, looked at me, and said "I always wanted to try this."

I only had a second to wonder what she meant when I felt her lips open around the head of my cock and slowly draw me inside. The thought of her mouth wrapped around my flesh and tasting our shared cum drove me mad. I closed my eyes and groaned loudly as she started to glide up and down the length of my cock. My senses were heightened and I felt the weight of her breasts sweeping over my thighs, her erect nipples grazing over my skin, and her long, luxurious hair swirling around my hips and balls. As she moaned with each thrust I felt myself move farther and farther from reality and nearer and nearer to another blissful climax. I was on that verge of not knowing if I wanted to come in her warm, deep mouth or submerge my cock deep into her cunt when she slowly withdrew my cock from her mouth, looked at me with those dark eyes like a panther on the prowl, and began to stalk up along my body. I surrendered to her passion as the darkness closed in upon me...

Felecia Barbaro
Working Overtime

Evan Thorne certainly was eccentric, I thought as I rang his doorbell. I couldn't figure out why he wanted to work on the Kilgore presentation at his home instead of the office. If it had been anyone else I would have suspected that a seduction was in the works. But this was Evan Thorne, the man who, according to my friend Muffin, was so cold he could chill a bottle of champagne just by touching it. He had never said more than "Good morning" to me since I joined Meacham & Co. six months ago. I wasn't sure he even knew my name. This would not be unusual for him. A long line of disappointed single women in the office could testify to his aloofness.

The front door opened, and there was Evan.

"Alison. Hi." His icy-blue eyes fixed right on mine.

Guess he did know my name, after all. "Hi, Evan."

God, he was gorgeous. This was not the first time that thought had crossed my mind. Six feet tall, lean and athletic, he seemed to fill the entire doorframe. His black wavy hair was somewhat mussed; I had the crazy urge to reach up and smooth it for him. *Get a grip, Alison,* I told myself. *Stay professional.* I had no desire to join the ever growing club of women who had humiliated themselves in front of Evan Thorne.

I couldn't help feeling a little awkward though. I had come straight from the office, still wearing my navy blue suit, beige pantyhose, and sensible black pumps, while he had changed into a gray sweatshirt, blue jeans and beat-up white Nikes. The sleeves of the sweater were pushed up, revealing muscular, tanned forearms. He looked as close to comfortable as I had ever seen him.

"I see you've got the Kilgore materials with you," he said, nodding at the bulging folder I carried under my arm. "I'm glad we could do this here instead of the office. It'll be more comfortable and there'll be fewer distractions. Why don't you come with me into the living room and we can get started."

Only Evan Thorne could make an invitation into the living room sound unsexy, I thought as I followed him.

Once in the living room, we seated ourselves on his comfortable overstuffed sofa and I turned down his offer of coffee. I opened the Kilgore folder and for the next hour and a half we immersed ourselves in data. The project, which looked so hopeless at nine a.m., was nearly done by nine p.m., and Evan was actually in a good mood. "Time for a break," he declared. He again offered me coffee and this time I accepted. He left the room and I shifted to a more comfortable position on the sofa, crossing my legs. I glanced at his coffee table and noticed that he had the latest issue of *The New Yorker*. I picked it up and began flipping through it. I quickly became engrossed in an article and I didn't hear Evan come back with the coffee.

"Do you take…"

The sound of his voice startled me. I looked up from the magazine and saw him standing frozen in the doorway, staring at me.

"Evan? Is everything okay?"

His face had turned a bright pink, and his breathing had noticeably quickened. He was carrying two steaming mugs, spoons, a creamer and a sugar bowl on a tray and I could see his white knuckles gripping the tray's edges. For a moment I thought he might be angry with me for touching his magazine. I quickly dropped it back onto the table.

But he wasn't staring at the magazine at all. I followed his gaze to my crossed legs and saw that one black pump was dangling off my foot. His eyes were riveted to my nylon-covered sole.

I quickly uncrossed my legs, slipping my foot back into the shoe. Evan shook his head and cleared his throat, his trance apparently broken.

"Uh. Sorry. Spaced out there for a moment." He uttered a self-deprecating chuckle and brought the tray over to the coffee table.

I muttered "Thank you" and reached for the sugar and milk. We sat there drinking the coffee for several minutes, neither of us speaking. I thought about what had just happened. During the six months I had worked with him and observed him, Evan had never blushed—he didn't seem like the blushing type. Nor was he given to "spacing out." Yet he had done both things, right after glimpsing my stockinged foot. Could he be a foot fetishist? The possibility was intriguing and definitely exciting. I had dated a foot lover a couple of years ago and I had loved using my feet to turn him on. I decided to try a few of those techniques on Evan and find out if he was indeed a foot man. Should be quite interesting, I thought.

I stretched my legs and frowned down at my feet. "These shoes sure do pinch," I grumbled.

"They do?" Was that a catch in Evan's voice or just my imagination?

"Yeah. They're brand new and a little tight. Usually I change into sneakers before I leave the office, but I was running late and I didn't have time tonight."

Evan's face flushed again. "Um—that's too bad," he muttered. "You could, uh…take them off, if you wanted."

I raised my eyebrows.

"You wouldn't mind?"

His cheeks were bright red now. "No, no, I don't mind at all. Why be uncomfortable?"

"Thanks, Evan. I really appreciate it." I set down my mug and slowly bent down. I took my time removing each shoe, slowly slipping it off my foot with a sigh of relief. Then I sat back on the couch, arching and flexing my feet, curling and wiggling my toes on the carpet. I turned to him with a smile. "Whew, that's much better."

"Good." His eyes were locked on my toes. I was glad I had painted the nails recently, because the bright red nail polish really stood out, even through the beige pantyhose.

I conspicuously wiggled my toes and rubbed my soles against the carpet, all the while uttering little moans and sighs of relief. Evan was practically drooling as he tried so hard to maintain his composure. I was really enjoying myself.

"My feet are so sore and tired at the end of the day," I said.

Evan cleared his throat. "Uh…maybe you'd like a foot rub? I'd be happy to give you one, if you wanted."

"You would? Oh, that sounds wonderful, Evan. Thank you so much."

He set down his mug and turned his body to face me. "Put your feet up."

I swung my legs up on the couch and scootched forward a little until my feet were in his lap. My skirt rode up a little on my thighs, but I made no attempt to pull it back down. Let him look if he wanted to.

He took my right foot in his large hands and began to rub it, applying gentle pressure all over the sole. "Do you like that?" he asked. His voice was a little hoarse.

"Mmmm, yeah." He worked my foot from the toes to the heel and then back again to the toes. He seemed to know every little pleasure point in the foot, and just how much pressure to apply to each of them. The sensations burned their way from my foot straight to my pussy. I squirmed with pleasure, feeling myself getting wet. I had forgotten how delightful a foot rub could be.

"You have lovely feet," he said. "These are the cutest feet I've seen in a long time. Such high arches. And the sole, so soft, not even a trace of a callus. And the toes…cute, chubby little toes…perfect, absolutely perfect." He spoke as if he were in a trance, rubbing all the time, staring hungrily down at my feet.

I decided to raise the stakes a little. As he rubbed away at my right foot, I slipped my left foot forward, gliding it up his thigh until I reached his crotch. No mistaking it. Evan was as hard as a rock and all because of my feet! He groaned as I gently probed the bulge with my toes.

"You like my feet, Evan?" I asked softly, moving my left foot in a gentle circular motion. "I've been wearing those awful shoes all day, so I'm sorry if they smell a little."

"Umm…no…they s-smell wonderful, Alison." And to my utter delight he picked up my right foot and pressed his nose to the nylon-covered sole. My clit throbbed as he inhaled deeply and then groaned.

"I've never seen you so…excited, Evan," I murmured. "I think I like this side of you."

Evan didn't respond. He was too busy holding my right foot in one hand so he could kiss it, while his free hand pressed down against my other foot, pushing it even more firmly against his hard on. His eyes closed as my toes wiggled on his bulge. I giggled at his boldness, but I couldn't deny that I was turned on. I pulled my skirt up a little more, then sneaked a hand underneath to finger my wet pantyhose crotch.

My soft moan made Evan open his eyes again. He gasped when he saw what I was doing to myself. I gave him my warmest smile and said: "Want to help me out, Evan?"

He didn't need any further encouragement. I removed my foot from his crotch as he quickly unzipped his jeans and released his cock. It was circumcised, about seven inches long, and nice and fat. I raised my butt a little and unzipped my skirt, then hooked my fingers in the waistband and pulled off the garment. Impatient now, I yanked down the panties and pantyhose, ripping a hole in the hose. Evan helped me pull them the rest of the way off, then held the pantyhose to his nose for another sniff before dropping them on the floor.

I crawled on top of him and gave him a long, deep kiss then slowly impaled myself on his hard cock. When he was fully inserted I paused for a long moment, savoring the feeling of fullness, enjoying Evan's tense, lust-filled expression. Then I began to move up and down, gradually picking up speed. I could feel my clit pulsing with every stroke and the long muscles in my thighs began to twitch. Evan's gasps and groans excited me unbearably.

It only took a few more strokes before I climaxed. My eyes squeezed shut and I made a low keening sound as the first waves of pleasure shook me. As if from a great distance I heard Evan groan, and then I felt him cumming inside me. We continued to thrust and grind, wringing every last bit of pleasure from each other, until we collapsed on the couch, completely satisfied.

When I'd recovered a little, I raised my head and looked at Evan. He met my gaze for a moment and then looked away. I climbed off him, retrieved my panties and skirt and pulled them back on. Evan remained where he was, slumped against the padded arm of the sofa. I sat down again and faced him, but he didn't look at me.

"Is this why you're so aloof in the office?" I asked, my voice soft. "You're embarrassed about your fetish?"

Evan sighed and rubbed his eyes.

"No, not embarrassed. I just don't want people to lose respect for me. 'Oh, there goes Evan Thorne, the guy who likes feet.' You know how people talk in that place."

"Yeah, I've heard the gossip."

"I can live with the gossip because I kind of like being the big mystery man," he said. He still didn't look at me. "I like to keep people guessing because it keeps them at a distance. What I'm afraid of is people finding out the truth and then ridiculing me. It happened to me in college. I finally worked up the courage to tell my girlfriend about my fetish and she couldn't handle it. Next thing I knew it was all over the campus. People were calling me "Toesucker" in the halls, stuff like that. It got so bad I had to transfer. I never told anyone why. I learned to be more careful over the years because not much has changed since then. Most people still think that having a fetish makes you a pervert."

I touched his knee. He finally looked me in the eye and the sadness on his face moved me.

"I don't think you're a pervert," I said. "I think you're a passionate man who's denied himself for far too long. I also think your old girl-friend was an immature little prig who missed out on a lot of pleasure. Her loss is my gain. I'd love to explore your fetish with you, if you want. And I will never breathe one word about it to anyone at the office. That's a promise."

He didn't react at first as my words sank in, then he smiled and let out a long sigh, as if he had finally put down a heavy weight he had been carrying.

"Oh my god," he said. "You don't know how long I've been waiting to meet someone like you. Perfect feet and perfect attitude. This is too good to be true. I just don't believe it."

"Believe it, Evan," I said with a smile. "Now what do you say we finish that project? And maybe tomorrow I can get you started on a brand-new project—like, say, giving me a pedicure?"

Anyone who saw Evan Thorne's face light up at that suggestion would never call him a cold fish again.

Stephen Van Scoyoc
A Handy Fuck

It may not sound like a very impressive title—handy man—but that's what I am at the Seawall Luxury Condominiums in Galveston. It's one of those things a writer will do to have the freedom to write. It's really a pretty sweet deal when you think about it. I have a tiny studio apartment on a top floor—which is enough for me—as one of the benefits. I also get to use the swimming pools, Jacuzzis, and tennis courts which are set among low rock walls, spraying fountains, and lush tropical foliage. Not to mention that the place is literally swarming with attractive women who were drawn to the security gates and 24 hour patrols. Mostly the women are single professionals who made it big working up in Houston. Now they drive Lexus cars, dress in the latest fashions, and generally have no use for men except for pleasure. It's given me more than a few stories to write about.

Oh—what do I write? That's easy. Erotica. By day I wear tidy, khaki coveralls with the name "John" stenciled over my pocket. I'm the guy who fixes the microwaves, seals the leaks, drives the nails, and wires the lights. By night though, I'm Richard Luskey, writer of erotica. I've even seen some of my books in the condos I work in. I always make a point of checking which pages have been folded. Sometimes I've even taken the risk of asking a woman what the books are about. Usually they just smile and blush, but other times—well—it's led to some interesting conversations and encounters!

"Ooops—there goes my pager."

"See Janet in 2B" my little screen said. I grabbed my toolkit and headed out the door into the sweltering summer heat. I was already sweating when I rang her door bell. Janet opened the door with a pearly smile and the bright sun flashed in her blue eyes. The blast of cold air escaping from her door was a welcome greeting and my skin prickled as the icy breeze cooled my sweaty skin. I stepped in and closed the door behind me.

I'd seen Janet around. She had just moved in a few weeks ago. Some corporate attorney I understood. She's like most of the women around here. Janet's in her thirties with dark, meticulously styled short hair framing a small, pleasant face. I usually see her in a dark business suit that covers all but her athletic legs, but today she was standing before me in white Nike trainers and wearing clingy cotton shorts beneath a light, cropped t-shirt. Her bare midriff was toned and set in her belly button was a gold stud with a blue sapphire shimmering in the light. Janet brushed some sweat from her brow with a small white towel and I noticed the stair-stepper in the corner. She had obviously been working out when I rang the door and her shirt was spotted with dark, wet patches around her neck and back, making the top cling even more enticingly to her well-sculpted body.

That's the thing about these professional women. No kids. No husbands. And bodies that look better than they did in college. I shifted a bit nervously as I felt my cock wake up and start to stretch out a bit. I was suddenly very aware that I wasn't wearing shorts under my coveralls, preferring the freedom of my skin against the loose uniform I'm expected to wear.

"I was just fixing some lemonade. Can I get you some too?" she asked in that soft, Texas drawl. I'm sure she was a vicious creature in the courtroom, but here she seemed nice and friendly.

"Yeah, that'll be great," I said thankfully. It was getting hotter in here than it was outside.

I heard the clatter of ice filling glass tumblers and looked around the room. It was first-rate, furnished in the best brands of furniture with original art on the walls and decorative Oriental figurines on the shelves and tables. I walked over and looked closely at the diplomas in their black lacquered frames. I recognized the schools, all really good ones, although I had turned down one of them for an even better one. Still, I never let on that I had my own collection of parchments in my tiny upstairs hovel. I always tried to notice these things about other people and use them in my stories to make them more realistic.

Janet handed me the tumbler of lemonade. It was already wet with drops of condensation and I took a long swallow of the cold juice while Janet looked up at me.

"Thanks, I really needed that."

Janet took one more tiny sip of hers, set her glass on the coffee table, and quickly stripped her t-shirt off. I was momentarily stunned and then realized she was wearing an Adidas exercise bra underneath. The black, stretchy fabric was a delicious contrast to her bronzed skin and it hugged her breasts in a way that made me envious. I was definitely having to think pure thoughts to prevent an embarrassing bulge in my uniform.

"I'm pretty much moved in, but there are some things that need to be done and I'm not very good with tools."

Oh, I've heard that line before. I just nodded and listened.

Janet picked up a bag and took out some large hooks that I recognized were for hanging bicycles from the ceiling. She handed them to me.

"I've got a mountain bike out in the garage that I like to ride on the beach, but it takes up too much room with the car and boxes. Can you put these up for me?"

"Yeah, no problem."

There were a few other things like shelves she wanted screwed into the wall and extra lights for the plants she was going to put on the shelves.

"When you're done I've got some curtain rods that need to be put up in my room. Just come in and yell for me. I'll be putting other things away."

"Okay," seemed like the only thing I needed—or was expected—to say.

Damn, she was a fine woman and I kept thinking about her as I sweated away in the stuffy garage. I admit I fantasized about taking those clothes off of her and stroking every inch of her smooth, tanned body. My coveralls were damp all over and my hair was soaked with perspiration. My cock was comfortably firm and each time it brushed against my wet coveralls an electric thrill passed through my body. I was just thinking about going in and asking for more lemonade—an excuse to see her again—when I heard her call out my name. I thought it sounded a bit different, but I couldn't quite put my finger on it.

"JOHN!" she repeated loudly. "Get up here—NOW!"

I thought she had hurt herself so I dropped what I was doing and raced into the house. I burst into Janet's room to find her standing there before a window. I stopped dead in my tracks. She was different somehow. She had changed into satiny shorts and a bright satiny ruby-red t-shirt. The earlier softness of her face now looked hard and angry.

"When the fuck are you going to put up this curtain rod?" she demanded.

I'm afraid I stumbled foolishly over my reply, stammering like a schoolboy in trouble with the teacher.

"I just had to change in front of this open window. There's no telling how many perverts out there watched me."

Remembering that the manager expected me to always treat the residents right I managed a simple reply.

"Yes ma'am. I'll take care of it right away."

I took some tools from my belt and began measuring the window and the curtain rod. It was one of those heavy wooden ones with brass rings. Damn, it was too long so I was going to have to cut it. I retrieved a saw from my toolkit in the garage and got to work on it while Janet watched me like a road gang overseer. As soon as my saw teeth bit into the wood I heard Janet sigh with exasperation.

"You fuckin' moron. You're getting dust all over my floor."

I tried to calm her down and assure her that I would clean up my mess. I could feel her eyes burning a hole into my back as I stretched up and began fastening the rod to the window frame. I was just taking the final turns with the screwdriver when I heard her harsh voice behind me again.

"What sort of handyman are you anyway. That's taking you forever—you'll never be finished with that!"

I bit my tongue and picked up the second rod, preparing to cut it.

"Oh great," she growled. "Now you're going…"

I didn't let her finish. I'd had enough of her crap. I was on top of her in a flash, straddling her with her arms pinned to her sides, and my weight pinning her to the soft bed. There was no way this tiny woman was going to escape from me. She opened her mouth in surprise and then prepared to scream, but I was ready for her. I plucked a few inches of duct tape from the roll on my belt and pressed it firmly over her mouth. Her eyes were wide as saucers and her nostrils flared in shock. Janet starting struggling, trying to free her arms, and violently thrusting her feet in an effort to topple me off of her.

I moved just enough to free her arms and quickly pinned her wrists together within one of my fists. My other hand skillfully wrapped several layers of duct tape around her wrists, restraining them securely. I slid further down her body, expecting her to try and sit up, which she did. The roll of tape was still on her wrists so in a few more seconds, like a spider entwining his prey, I had wrapped it around her waist, pinning her arms and hands tightly to her belly. She was starting to look more worried than angry and I had already gone too far to turn back.

I forced Janet back down onto the bed, rolled her over, turned around, and repeated the process with her legs. I stepped away with some real satisfaction and looked at Janet securely bound upon her own bed. I wasn't sure what to do next as I looked at her breathing heavily and testing the strength of her bonds. Her eyes followed my every movement as I returned to the curtain rod I had started working on before her tantrum. I finished cutting it to length, taking my time, and fastened it to the brackets above the window.

Janet had started whimpering quietly and I turned to look at her. The sight of her curvy body was enough to reawaken the cravings my cock had felt for her earlier. Her eyes lowered to the rather pointed lump in my coveralls and I decided then and there to go for broke. I strode across the room, bent over, and roughly threw Janet up onto my shoulder. She grunted as my arm gripped her forcefully. I walked back out into the garage. It was even hotter than before and the perspiration started streaming off of me as soon as I closed the door behind me. I looked around and had an idea. I dropped Janet, a little roughly, onto the hood of her Jaguar and bent over to rummage in my tool box for a sturdy length of rope. I found just what I was looking for—some poly rope that I used to hold building materials on the top of my car.

I turned back to Janet. She was looking at the strong hooks I had screwed into the ceiling for her bicycle. Well, at least she was thinking along my lines! I slid her gently off the car and onto her feet. Reaching into my belt I took out my razor knife and clicked the shiny blade out menacingly. Janet's eyes opened wide again as I swiftly cut the tape holding her arms fast to her waist. I gripped her still bound wrists and tied one end of the rope snugly over the tape. Reaching up, I draped the loose end over the hook in the ceiling and stretched it tight, raising Janet's arms high above her head. Then I stretched it just a bit higher so she had to stretch to keep her balance. The other end I fastened securely to the pouncing cat on the bonnet of her car. I stepped back to survey my handiwork. Janet was still and quiet, her eyes locked on me, watching my every move.

Janet winced when I clicked the blade of my knife out to its full length. I stepped toward her and she began to struggle and whimper at my advance.

"Hold still you nasty little bitch!" I commanded her. She stopped immediately.

The blade sliced effortlessly through the expensive fabric of her t-shirt. It dropped away onto the floor at my feet like a rag. Janet was wearing a filmy brassiere of lace and nylon which hugged the delicious softness of her breasts. Dark brown nipples pressed teasingly against the wet fabric and I felt my erection surge even harder. I resisted the temptation to stroke her and sliced through the bra with more of the same ease. With her hands held high above her head and her body stretched taut her breasts formed small, firm mounds of flesh which rose and fell with her breathing. Tiny drops of perspiration beaded up and rolled down her chest and onto the swell of her breasts. The bra fell in a tangled heap of straps and lace onto the hard concrete floor. I knelt down on my knees and sliced through her shorts and matching panties to reveal the gentle swell of her hips and her tight waist. Janet's cunt hair was neatly trimmed to hide behind the fashionable swimsuit I had seen her wearing at the pool. A small tuft of dark hair, like that on her head, decorated the soft flesh nestled between her legs. I could see that her lips were swelling just like my cock. I wondered if she was actually enjoying this as much as me.

Again I stepped back to look at my prisoner. A thin, shiny sheen of sweat layered her body. It was fully tanned and toned. Her legs were slim yet muscular. The only thing she was still wearing was the sapphire jewel in her navel. She was a gorgeous and desirable creature.

"You've been a very naughty girl! You had no right to talk to me like you did," I chided her.

Janet tried to mumble behind the tape over her mouth, but I ignored her.

"I'll bet nobody has ever punished you properly," I remarked as I reached into my belt and pulled out my tape measure. I extended it a few inches to expose the tip of it. Stepping nearer to Janet I touched her neck with the end of the blade and started to draw the end of it down the length of her body, between her breasts, and toward her cunt. Janet squeezed her thighs tightly together, closed her eyes, and sighed noticeably through her nose. I started at her neck again, this time tracing a line over her breasts, and letting the stop of the blade snag on her nipple, tugging roughly at it. Janet's nipples both hardened at the touch. By now Janet was moving slightly, trying to guide the cold metal closer to her pleasures. With a loud snap I let the tape wind back into the measure. Janet's eyes popped open in surprise. I unclasped my tool belt and let it drop to the floor. Then I unzipped my coveralls and let them slide down the length of my sweaty body to gather on the floor.

I reached into my toolbox and withdrew a two foot long metal ruler. I pressed the cool flat metal to her ass and stroked it against her skin in small circles. Then I drew back and landed a sharp swat on her rounded ass. Janet let out a muffled cry as an angry red welt rose on the cheek of her ass. I again stroked the flat steel against her skin for a few seconds before smacking her again with a loud crack. Janet's cries became deep moans and she writhed in anticipation of each blow against her tender skin. Her ass was a bright red as I prepared to land one or two more swats for punishment. As the echoes died away from the final blows, Janet's body tightened up. I could hear the rope creaking from her weight as her body began to shudder all over. Her face grimaced and contorted as she let out a long guttural moan of orgasm. I was entranced by this erotic display. I thought I could see a smile appear behind the gray tape covering her mouth.

Janet suddenly looked so peaceful that I leant down and took her nipple into her mouth. I was instantly rewarded by a moan. I swallowed more of her flesh into my mouth. My hands caressed her hips and waist before wrapping around her to stroke the burning flesh of her ass. The tape binding Janet's legs had loosened enough that my fingers could press between her legs, into the moist warmth depth of her cunt. Janet pressed herself insistently against my teasing fingers. One of my fingers found its way between the swollen, silky lips and pressed deep inside of Janet. Her body shuddered once again in orgasm and I could feel my cock quickly respond with hunger. I pulled away from Janet and heard her whine with complaint, but I had other plans.

Untying the rope from the Jaguar's hood ornament, I lowered Janet's aching arms to her waist and used the rope to bind them tightly to her tummy. I spied her fingers digging deeply into her cunt and stroking herself. I picked her up and laid her down on the bonnet of the Jag, with her head over the chrome trim of the grille.

"I'll uncover you mouth if you promise not to scream."

Janet nodded dreamily.

I tried to pull the tape from her face as gently as possible, but she didn't seem to mind. As soon as the tape was free I slipped my swollen cock into Janet's mouth. Janet couldn't move, but I stroked my cock in and out, fucking her willing mouth as we both moaned. I knew I couldn't last long and the closer I got to cumming the more excited Janet seemed to get. I took one more look at her tanned body curled up on the long green bonnet of the Jag and thrust in deeply. My cum filled her mouth and she eagerly continued to suck hard on my cock and swallow nearly all of my cum. I almost collapsed onto the floor from the intensity. I weakly pulled away from her and noticed her fingers were again buried between her legs while louder and louder groans slipped from the same mouth that had just sucked me dry. In seconds she was thrusting her hips and straining her neck into an arch.

As she lay there moaning softly I shrugged back into my coveralls and began to gather my tools up. When I was finished I reached over and untied her wrists. Using the knife I sliced the tape on her wrists. Janet pulled the tape free and massaged her red skin. I set the knife on the edge of the bonnet and looked at her.

"If you want me to finish the job you know the number," I said gruffly.

I pushed the button for the garage door and watched it slowly open up. Sunlight flooded the dim garage. I turned one last time to see Janet still laying on the bonnet, naked, eyes glazed, and partly bound.

I walked straight to my own condo, wondering if I was about to find myself without a job—or worse. I sat down at my desk and began to scribble furiously. Even if I lost my job at least I had one hell of a story to tell. I had only written a few lines when my damned pager went off. I pushed the button to display the message, fearing the worst.

"Please see Janet in 2B. She has some more work for you."

"Selene"

The Prostitute

The night was chilly and damp. I wasn't dressed for it but at first I hardly noticed the weather. I stood at a street corner in Chapeltown and, looking at my watch, I could see it was just past ten o'clock. I had a long night ahead of me. The cobbles shone wetly and black, with orange lights and street signs reflected in the puddles and mist haloing the streetlamps. I teetered on five-inch heels, to which I was unaccustomed, worried that any false step could send me sprawling into the gutter. I'd tried the shoes on earlier, at home, and seen how they affected the way I stood—forcing me onto tiptoe, my bottom thrust out, my breasts held high, to achieve that precarious balance. It had been hard enough to walk on the smooth surface of my kitchen lino. Now I had maybe six hours or so ahead of me—although of course, I didn't expect to be standing up all that time…

I'd tried on the whole outfit earlier that day for the first time. You'd brought it 'round, you'd chosen every item, none of which I'd ever seen before. It wasn't the sort of thing I'd ever have worn normally, not even to a party—well, maybe to a tarts and vicars do, but actually I'd probably have gone as a female vicar. The clothes I had on consisted of a tacky black PVC halter-neck top which zipped up the front as far as the plunging neckline; a red lace suspender-belt and seamed black stockings, and over that, a microscopically short, black leather miniskirt with a zip all the way up one side—a zip, you'd informed me, which was to remain fully open at all times. Not that it made much difference—the skirt was so short that it cleared my stocking-tops by a couple of inches anyway and little, very little, was left to the imagination.

I had to admit that I rather liked the way the skin-tight PVC halter-neck supported my tits and gave me an impressive cleavage. If it had been made of less cheap material it could have looked quite stunning. As it was, the overall effect of the outfit—finished by those cliff-edge five inch red stilettos—was tawdry, sleazy and cheap. As a rule I didn't wear much make-up but tonight was an exception. If nothing else, it was a mask to hide behind. It was highly unlikely that anyone who knew me would be passing through Chapeltown—and no-one who did would think to recognise the ordinary housewife they knew in the painted whore loitering for a client on the street corner.

You'd bought me the pitch for the night—otherwise there's no way I'd have been allowed to stand there, plying a trade that was to be my calling for the night—for just one night. You'd even fixed me up a room nearby, so that I could take any clients back who wanted to pay the extra. But you'd warned me that most of my business would take place right there on the street. My instructions were simple. I was to stand there until you came to fetch me and I was to take all comers. Half an hour had passed and apart from one or two other girls further down the street, Chapeltown seemed deserted. Of course it was early yet—the pubs were still full. Come chucking-out time, things would be different.

You'd dropped me off early so that the full enormity of what I was about to undertake would have time to sink in. Earlier it hadn't seemed real—it was just a game. Now the initial adrenaline surge was beginning to wear off and I began to feel the chill of the evening striking into my inadequately covered flesh. I clasped my arms about me, envying the girl I could see about fifty yards away, in her short but cosy fur coat. You'd smiled slyly when I'd asked what I was to wear over the top of my outfit. "You'll do as you are," you'd said. "The cold will give you an incentive to work hard." When you'd arrived with the clothes and told me what I was to do tonight, I'd felt a thrill of undeniable excitement mixed in with the fear. You knew, of course, because I'd told you, that acting as a prostitute for the night was one of my favourite fantasies and of course we'd acted the scenario out between us many times. But this was different—this was on another level entirely. This was the real thing and it had never occurred to me that I'd ever actually be in the position I was now in.

But here I was, and what was more, I was here with your blessing. More even than that, I was under orders. I couldn't refuse this experience whether I thought I wanted to or not. You'd given me this chance as if conferring a privilege on me—this was a gift from you to me, albeit a gift of a strange kind. I wondered too how you felt about sharing me with any number of strangers. This too was new territory for us. Occasionally, you'd made me perform for various of your friends and acquaintances, but always under your direct control. Tonight I was at the whim of a host of unknowns. I might pick up one or two punters or possibly a legion of them—I had no way of knowing exactly what lay ahead.

I was so busy mulling these thoughts over, turning the implications round and around in my head that I almost missed my first punter altogether. He'd come right up to me and was even now taking hold of my arm and motioning with his head around the corner into the alleyway between the back-to-backs.

"Not seen you around before," he said.

"No, I'm new," I answered and he smiled.

"You'll be busy tonight then, love," he commented, pushing me into a doorway and undoing his flies.

"Ten pounds for a wank, twenty for a blow-job, forty for a fuck," I said, not absolutely sure what the going rates were but not really caring either.

He produced a couple of ten-pound notes, which I stuffed down the front of my halter-neck top, and pushed me to my knees on the cobbles.

I had a split-second vision of myself as I must appear to an observer, as I took this unknown man's cock into my mouth. I could hardly believe I was doing it yet in another way it seemed the most natural thing in the world. It was a simple act, after all, and one I'd performed countless times in the past. When you're down there on your knees a cock is just a cock and bar some exceptionally unusual ones, any cock could be attached to any body really. Or so I reasoned in that split-second before I had to stop thinking and concentrate on the job in hand.

Funnily enough, it took much less time than I'd expected. I rather prided myself on the quality of my blow job technique, but this man wasn't interested in a virtuoso performance. He just wanted to come and after only a couple of minutes thrusting fairly roughly in and out of my mouth, come he did, grunting as if in pain as he shot a decent load of cum down my throat. Judging by the quantity and the speed of his response, it had been a fair while since his last orgasm. He pulled away from me and did up his flies. With a muttered "Goodnight, love" he set off back into the main street and I got to my feet, slightly unsteadily and almost light-headed with relief.

I'd just survived my first encounter, it had been a success and I'd lived to tell the tale. In fact it had been relatively easy really. Perhaps I was a natural. Walking gingerly I picked my way back across the cobbles to the main street. I glanced at my watch. The entire incident had lasted barely fifteen minutes. I felt high on adrenaline. I no longer felt cold. I stood on my pitch more confidently, even though I stood alone. The other girls might tolerate me for the night, they knew the score, but I wasn't one of them and they kept their distance. I didn't care. I felt wrapped in my task as if in a protective blanket. I wanted to be alone, so that I could experience it as clearly and cleanly as possible—no distractions.

My second client appeared and again I found myself on my knees on the cobbles. Only my second man yet already I felt as if I'd been doing this for years. This one was less prepossessing than my first—he smelt, he had a huge beer gut, his clothes looked like he slept in them. He didn't talk much but held my head so closely as he thrust his cock in and out of my mouth that I was stifled. I wished he'd hurry up and come but he was slower than the first one too. My jaws ached and my temples throbbed with pressure. I was trying to breathe through my nose but what with his body and the way he held me it was difficult. I slipped my fingers between his legs, massaging his balls with one hand while pressing hard, suddenly, on his perineum with the other. This did the trick and brought him to orgasm, but he pulled back as he came and shot his cum all over my face.

I wasn't sure what etiquette was in this sort of case. Maybe he even thought he'd done me a favour, not coming in my mouth. He looked down at me, the spunk dripping off my nose and chin, plastered all over my cheek, gleaming orange in the sodium light from the streetlamp down the way. He grinned.

"Lick it," he said and dutifully I put out my tongue and licked off what I could. "You're a good sport," he said. "I'll look out for you again."

And with that he vanished into the night. Subdued, I got to my feet, wiping what remained of his cum off my face with the back of my hand. I had nothing with me to repair the damage to my make-up and already I could feel the tightness as his cum dried on my skin. This had some-how been different to the first encounter. It couldn't just be because of the unattractiveness of the man—I hadn't found the first one attractive after all—but this had been different.

Perhaps it was just that it was beginning to dawn on me that I really did have no choice in the matter. No choice—those words were a pow-erful charm to me. So many times I'd heard them and every time they were uttered by you I felt a rush of juice in my cunt as the charm worked its magic in my mind. Yet almost always the matter in which I had no choice was one in which I didn't want any choice anyway. You took away my freedom in order to free me to do those things that, when I was free, I didn't have the nerve to demand. It was a paradox but one we both understood and used to our mutual advantage. Now once again I had no choice, but I felt less in control and more worrying, I wasn't sure that you were in control either. But I shook my head free of that unworthy thought. Of course you were in control. I hobbled back to my corner, my knees bruised from the cobbles, holes in my stockings. What with that and my face, I was looking somewhat the worse for wear and now, I realised, the streets were suddenly full—the pubs had emptied of their clientele and my night was about to begin in earnest.

The next couple of hours passed in a blur. I lost track of the numbers of men I serviced. Almost every one of them simply wanted a blowjob and I would hardly make it back to the main street, my mouth still full of the taste of the previous client, before the next had hurried me back around the corner and was undoing his flies while I crouched on the cold, wet stones at his feet. The stack of notes in my halter-neck top was growing. I stopped thinking about the men—the job became entirely mechanical at this stage. My face ached as never before, the amount of cum in my stomach made me sick to think of it, any glamour the job had had for me had vanished long ago, round about the time my fourth punter had followed his orgasm—another in-my-face number—with a few swift and hard slaps and harder words.

My eyes had filled with tears but I told myself he was a sad bastard and anyway, he had a very small dick which probably explained everything. I was quite surprised when occasionally a fuck was called-for—then I extricated a condom from a small pouch under my skirt but so far, the one or two men who'd wanted sex had settled for a quick knee-trembler in the alley, pressing me back—or forwards—against a doorway. That had been better than the endless succession of blow-jobs—for a start my legs were protesting at all the time spent on my knees on the unforgiving cobbles—and it made for a break from swallowing jet after jet of come.

Around one o'clock there was another lull and I actually made it back onto the street this time without meeting any prospective client on the way. My legs were actually trembling with exhaustion by this time—partly it was all the kneeling and partly it was the strain of those damn heels. I just wasn't used to them and it felt like a heavy task in its own right just trying to balance and walk in them. I knew I must look a mess by now and when the car pulled up beside me, although I didn't recognise it, at first I wondered if it was you come to take me home. I would have gone happily, relieved the night was over. It was perfectly possible that you'd be in a strange car—I assumed you'd been keeping an eye on me all night, one way or another.

But it wasn't you I saw as I stepped up to the wound-down window. The man inside asked me to get in and take him to my room for a fuck. I looked around quickly, trying to see you. Of course I couldn't and you'd prepared for this eventuality so I assumed you'd be watching over me. Nevertheless, getting into that car felt incredibly dangerous and my admiration for the women who made this their daily work increased in leaps and bounds. Once in the car I relaxed a little, because the man who was driving had an open, friendly sort of face with a distinct twinkle in his eye.

"Where to, love?," he asked and I gave him directions—in fact the room was only a couple of hundred yards away, but I had to admit, it was blissful sitting down if only for a few minutes.

I was pleased to be able to take stock at last and start thinking again instead of merely functioning as a physical receptacle for all these men's most basic needs. The man I was about to fuck must have been in his mid-fifties. He was on the stout side but quite powerfully-built—like a man who'd prided himself on his body in his youth but who now had let go rather. He was balding and about the same height as me in my stilettos, so not very tall. But there was something about him—a certain physical ease and confidence. I was glad he'd opted to come back to the room. Something of my initial excitement returned. I led the way upstairs and unlocked the door. The room was simply-furnished to say the least. There was a double bed, spread with a sheet alone; a chair and small chest-of-drawers; a frayed rug on top of old green lino; and a wash-basin; but it was clean and the gas fire was already on, burning on its lowest setting, so the place was warm and seemed very welcoming, to my cold and weary bones at any rate.

He sat on the bed and unlaced his boots, then looked up at me.

"Let's see you strip then love," he said.

Strange, after so many men that night, this was the first time I'd actually had to undress. For a moment I felt like a novice all over again. Then I thought, what the hell, it's warm here and he seems nice enough—the longer he stays with me here, the longer 'till I have to go back out on the streets.

Slowly, I inched the zipper down on the halter-neck top. In fact the zip was more decorative than functional—the way to get out of the top was to release the clips behind my neck and waist—but I was going to make this a show he'd remember. However, I'd forgotten about all the money I'd stuffed down there during the course of the evening. Suddenly, as the zip inched below a critical point, showers of tenners fluttered out and fell all over the floor. The man on the bed roared with laughter and I blushed as I stooped down to pick them all up as quickly as I could. As I bent down, of course my breasts fell out of the top and what had been going to be a slow and elegant strip was dangerously near descending into farce.

My client was now wiping tears of mirth from his eyes. Although mortified at first, I couldn't help suddenly seeing the funny side myself and as I shoved all the money into the chest-of-drawers a giggle escaped me too. I sat down suddenly on the bed beside him, too weak in the knees with laughter and weariness for my legs to support me.

"It's clear you're not an expert at this," my client said when he'd regained his composure, although he was still grinning broadly.

"You're right," I admitted. 'It's the first time I've ever done anything like this really."

"Why start now?" he asked, clearly intrigued.

"It's a long story, you don't want to hear really," I said.

"Try me," he said.

Well, orders are orders. I wasn't about to go into my entire sexual history but I had to come up with something that was as near to the truth as possible.

"OK," I said, "if you really want to know—I always fancied having a go at this and—well, my boyfriend dared me—so this is a one-off, tonight. I'm doing it for a dare."

His eyes widened as he took in what I'd said. Then he expelled his breath in a long slow whistle.

"Well, well, well," he said. "I've struck lucky tonight and no mistake. A woman who's doing it for the love of the thing—that's a rare commodity, that is."

He thought for a moment, drumming his fingers on his knees.

"You'll carry on with the strip and we'll fuck," he said. "But I'm just going to call a couple of my friends. You've no objection I take it? Come one come all?"

I thought for a split-second. This possibility hadn't occurred to me but after all, why not? You'd told me to take all comers and if they came three-at-a-time, what of it? Furthermore—my mouth curved in a smile—Maybe more than just one of my fantasies was about to be realised tonight.

He asked me the address and I was glad I'd made a mental note of it when you'd shown me the room earlier that day. He made a couple of calls on his mobile and I had visions of men waking blearily in their marital beds and being summoned to an orgy with no prior warning. I couldn't help wondering whether they thought it was a wind-up but my client didn't seem to worry about disturbing them at this late hour. And if he wasn't worried, there was no reason why I should be. He smiled when he put his phone away.

"We should have plenty of time to ourselves first," he commented. "I'd like to have you all to myself for a bit—but this is something I had to share."

He jerked his head at me—a clear gesture that told me it was time to get on with the strip. While he'd been speaking on the phone I'd pulled my zipper up a bit so that I could start again and make a better attempt at it this time. The earlier fiasco and our subsequent chat had cemented some sort of bond between us. We seemed less like prostitute with client now and more like sexual partners. I hardly knew this man but felt that he was someone who in other circumstances I'd get along well with. I felt relaxed with him now and that showed in my movements as I rose to my feet, sashayed around to stand in front of him and teasingly began to lower my zipper once more.

I kept my movements slow and seductive, swaying my hips as I balanced in those criminally-high heels, and freed my breasts with a flourish. I tossed the PVC halter-neck onto the chair and caressed my breasts lovingly. It felt good, the air on them after they'd been sweatily bound in plastic for all these hours. I teased my nipples with my fingertips, hardening them, using my hands cupped around my breasts to show them off—after all, they were one of my best features in most men's eyes. My friend, as I had begun to think of him, smiled appreciatively and I leant towards him, offering him them to suck. I only let him have the merest lick before pulling away again and then, holding his gaze with my own, I bent my head and lifted my left breast to my own lips. I sucked the nipple into my mouth and chewed gently on the end. It felt good and I knew he enjoyed seeing me do this. But I was conscious of time slipping away and stepped back again. It was time to get on with the strip.

Next to go was my skirt—all I had to do was unhook the catch that held it in place around my waist—but I held onto the waistband with both hands after I'd undone it, conscious that once I let it fall he'd be able to see my cunt and, not wanting to reveal all to him immediately, I turned my back and held the skirt—now one rectangle of leather—wide, and as if it was a towel with which I was drying myself, I rubbed my arse against it. Then I lowered my arms slowly, slowly, inching the skirt down so that more and more of my arse was revealed to him—as was the fact, if he hadn't guessed it already, that I wasn't wearing knickers. Now it was the turn of the skirt to be thrown neatly onto the chair as I stood there clad only in my narrow red suspender-belt, black stockings and red shoes. I knew my back view must be delightful, my round arse framed in red lace and black nylon. My friend certainly seemed to think so—I could hear him clearing his throat.

I stepped out of the shoes, turning around to face him as I did so. The fact that I was now several inches shorter and that my legs wouldn't look so good would be more than offset by the sight of my naked, clean-shaven cunt, the gold of the ring in my clit hood gleaming at the point where my labia flowered from my mons. Standing closer to him, my cunt at his eye-level, I put a foot up beside him on the bed. He could now see right inside me if he wanted to. My cunt, not at all to my surprise, was feeling distinctly juicy and open and, as I undid the suspenders on that leg, I could smell the delicious scent of my own sex. Keeping my leg up, my thigh almost brushing his cheek, I unrolled the stocking and drew it off my leg. Then I repeated the operation with my other leg. I moved even closer so that this time he could hardly help but bury his nose in my cunt.

Deftly I unhooked the suspender belt and dropped it onto the floor. My friend pressed his face into my cunt, inhaling my scent, which luckily was all mine—the rubbery smell of the condoms the other clients had used now well hidden under the intoxicating perfume of my own moisture. I caressed the back of his neck, pressing his face further into me and moving my hips against him. This was definitely more like it. This was how I'd imagined it could be. He put his hands on my waist and gently but firmly put me from him.

"Time I got my own kit off," he said, and undressed quickly, laying his clothes neatly on the chair. I'd stretched out on the bed and it was no time at all before he joined me. I wasn't sure whether to take the lead or let him choose how we fucked. All I knew was that for the first time that night I was actually turned on by the client himself and the things we were doing. Before, it had been the idea of what they were doing to me—the use to which I was being put. The men could have been anyone. Were indeed anyone. But this was different.

Fleetingly I wondered if my desire to fuck this man counted as unfaithfulness to you but no, it couldn't be. We both knew what things were likely to happen to me and that one way or another I would take pleasure in those things. That had been your intention, after all. That, plus your own pleasure in knowing that I would do this, would indeed do anything, for you, unquestioningly. It never ceased to amaze and gratify me that we'd found each other—I who took pleasure in such esoteric things and you, who wanted me to do them and found your own pleasure thereby.

He moved close to me and stroked his fingers over my cunt, tugging gently at the ring, which caused ripples of pleasurable sensation to surge through me. His fingers explored, smoothing over my nakedness, spreading me open as they went, dipping just inside my cunt, discovering me and tantalising me at one and the same time. This wasn't a casual fuck. This was making love. He leant over and kissed me. I knew prostitutes weren't in the habit of kissing their clients but this was different and I opened my mouth to his. His lips were surprisingly gentle and soft and he actually kissed rather well. His mouth tasted good and I gave myself up to the kiss, feeling more and more turned on by this man. As his teeth closed playfully over my lower lip, I felt his cock sliding into my cunt at last. I gasped at the rightness of the feeling and wrapped my legs around his body.

Slowly at first, he moved in and out of me, long deliberate strokes that each time made me fear he intended to withdraw altogether but controlled so that he never did. Gradually he built the rhythm up so that he was fucking me harder and faster. I was fucking him back, clasping my cunt muscles around him, trying to give him as much pleasure as he was giving me. He moved so that he was almost kneeling, and lifted my legs high, holding my ankles up in one strong hand so that I was bent back on myself and he could watch his cock sliding, more slowly now, in and out of me. I couldn't see, of course, but suddenly it occurred to me that I hadn't put a condom on him and I didn't know if he'd put one on himself. I assumed that he would have done, out of a sense of self-preservation if nothing else.

He moved again so that my ankles were resting on his shoulders and leant forwards so that I was doubled-up underneath him. Now he moved harder and faster, harder and faster, knocking the breath out of me with each delicious stroke. Thoughts of condoms, all thoughts of any kind, vanished as I gave myself up to the man and the act, the all-encompassing sensations that were building in my body. Suddenly, he stopped, pulling back slightly.

"I don't want to come just yet," he muttered. "I'll wait—save it till the others get here."

Slowly, he withdrew from me and I lowered my legs to the bed. My cunt, dripping wet, ached to be filled once more. Instead, we lay next to each other, tracing the lines of our bodies, exploring the textures, hills and hollows with our fingers and the tastes of skin, salt and slick with sweat, with our tongues. We caught each others' gazes and laughed, almost guiltily. Surely it wasn't actually supposed to be this good.

That, at least, was what I was thinking when the knock came at the door. "Company," he said with a smile, and smacked me lightly on the arse. "Get up, woman, and let them in."

Naked, I rose from the bed and opened the door to the two men who stood there slightly awkwardly. My friend raised himself on one elbow and called them into the room.

"We didn't wait for you," he said with a grin, "but there's plenty to go around. Better get undressed - I should..."

He didn't make introductions but I hardly expected that—it would have been difficult anyway as he didn't know my name. His friends stripped, laying their clothes neatly on top of his and mine on the chair and I could hardly help noticing that both of them were already hard and obviously eager to join the fray.

Both the newcomers were younger than him, although only one appeared to be younger than I was and he was a really handsome-looking young man in his early twenties, too young for me—I always preferred older men—but then again, too gorgeous to resist, not that resisting was on the cards tonight no matter what they looked like. This young man had tanned skin, as if he worked outdoors, stripped to the waist, in all weather. He had thick, floppy chestnut hair worn long on top but shaved into the nape of his neck—a nape that just begged to be caressed. In fact he had rather the look of a glossy-maned pony, you wanted to stroke him.

The older man was about my own age, maybe a little older, also tanned and his dark hair, close-cropped, was grizzled. He had deep-set green eyes and I felt a lurch of lust deep within when our glances met.

Heavens, what was happening to me tonight? I felt insatiable. I'd already performed sexual acts with more men in this one night than in my entire life up 'till now and yet here I was, wanting even more. I shook my head with a little laugh. Going back to everyday life would perhaps seem rather tame after this. There was little time for reflection after that. Soon we were all on the bed together—I hoped it was strong enough—and tangled up in a mess of limbs and parts and hair and hands so that it was impossible for me to tell which bit belonged to which man and really it hardly seemed to matter. They made sure no one of them missed out. At first we were just touching and stroking and feeling each other, using hands and mouths to touch and lick, kiss and bite, stroke and pinch, in a barrage of sensation that was exquisite in its unpredictability.

Wherever I laid my hands or mouth, an eager cock found its target, or a mouth closed around my fingers, or my breasts. I sucked and kissed and nibbled and stroked each of them, as they constantly moved around me and in turn, no part of my body was left unkissed, unlicked, untouched. My cunt was spilling its juices down my thighs and always there was a tongue there licking them up. Fingers probed my arse, my cunt, my mouth, my ears even. Our legs and arms entwined and it was impossible to tell where one body ended and one began or, in the end, whose pleasure was the greater. Finally, someone's cock penetrated my cunt and as we rocked together, blind with lust, another cock fed itself into my mouth. I was unaware of who was fucking me or who I was sucking, I'd closed my eyes the better to give myself up to physical sensation.

I was sitting astride, circling my hips, controlling the pace at which we fucked. The man I was impaled upon was of a good size, but I was so wet and open that it was hard to keep him within me. Then I felt a gentle pressure on my neck as I was pushed forward. I opened my eyes to see that the man I was fucking was the gorgeous youngster, and as I was pushed further down my breasts dangled into his face. He took one of my nipples into his mouth and closed his own eyes in a beatific expression of satisfaction as he chewed on my nipple, almost smothered by my breasts. The man I was sucking lowered himself to his knees, the joints cracking like pistol-shots, and I recognised the man who'd claimed my attention in the first place. That meant that the man whose cock was even now pressing gently but firmly against my arsehole was the man with the beautiful eyes, the one who'd made my stomach flip over when I'd first taken a look at him.

I relaxed my muscles, making the entry as easy for him as possible. He knew what he was doing and evidently didn't want to hurt me—he took his time—his cock hard but only inching forward as he penetrated me slowly, so slowly that I hardly felt the moment that he slipped inside. The feeling was almost indescribable. I'd never felt so full in my life. I couldn't concentrate on what was happening. One moment more conscious of the cock in my mouth, then the one in my cunt, then the one in my arse—it seemed impossible to comprehend the totality of sensation, as if my brain and body were overloaded and could not cope with the full experience. But although my brain was shutting down my body seemed to be taking over. I'd given up on trying to control anything that was happening now. The men were setting their own rhythm and all I had to do was to give myself up to them utterly. I felt like a rag doll, let myself go limp so as not to interfere with the beat of our bodies.

The man beneath me could take no more, what with my own writhing as I was thrust into by the man behind me and the extra stimulation that thrusting was giving him. He shuddered and stiffened as he came, pumping his cock into me with all the vigour you'd expect in a man his age. The man in my arse stepped up his rhythm and fucked me harder and faster. Although he'd used nothing but my own juices to lube me with I was so wet and open now that it felt to me that he was sliding in and out almost as easily as if it were into my cunt. Meanwhile my old friend was still holding out, admirably, at my mouth, determined to last at least as long as his younger colleagues. The man I still sat astride was softening slowly inside me and in fact this made the vigorous arse-fucking I was still receiving more pleasurable—I was no longer stretched almost beyond my capacity.

Nevertheless I felt on the verge of collapse and would have allowed myself to sink onto my stomach if it hadn't been for my old friend still availing himself of my mouth. I put all my efforts now into pleasuring him. The others could take care of themselves. I looked up at my friend and smiled at him as well as I could around his cock. I did my best to alternate long wet licks with sucking and nibbling although it was hard to control my actions with the man behind me now holding me tightly at the hips and thrusting into me more and more quickly as he built towards his climax. The sight of this coupled with my closer attention however, proved too much now for the older man and at last he came, his cock unleashing copious amounts of cum into my mouth and down my throat.

This sudden outpouring into my mouth tipped me over the edge into my own orgasm—the first in that long night, but one which had been building in me slowly, little by little but inexorably, almost from the moment you'd arrived at my front door hours earlier with my now-discarded tart's clothes in your hands. Slowly as it had arrived, drawing upon sensations such as I'd never experienced before and emotions stirred deeply by the behaviour you'd forced me into during the course of the past few hours, behaviour which answered some deeply-felt need that 'till now had never truly been met, now it crashed upon me with the full force of a tidal wave. It felt as if I'd never come before, as if this was a totally new way of feeling, stronger and more moving and devastating than any orgasm I'd ever experienced in my life up 'till now. Totally abandoned to the moment and my physical being, I moaned and thrashed and my body jerked over and over in spasms of pleasure so sharp they were almost like pain... All of which was far too much for the man in my arse and, crying out as if he too was in pain, he came inside me, clinging onto my body as if to something solid in a stormy sea.

I certainly felt as if I'd been overtaken by nothing less than shipwreck or earthquake or flood. Waves of sweeter, lesser pleasure were still washing over me as I slipped down onto the bed, my muscles still clenching and unclenching rhythmically. It seemed like the longest orgasm I'd had in my entire life. All four of us lay there, drained, slippery with sweat which cooled rapidly now on our relaxed bodies. Perhaps we slept—certainly we lay there in companionable silence, replete, while we gathered our wits and our strength. My old friend, finally, was the first to make a move.

"It's three in the morning, friends," he said. "Time we were on our way."

He turned to look at me as he pulled on his clothes. "What about you, love?" he asked. "What now for you?"

What indeed, I wondered dully. I supposed I had to dress and go back out onto the streets—a prospect which was anything but pleasing at that late hour, in my current state of blissed-out exhaustion, in that cold, damp night.

"I'll drop you off," he said and at his words the others were galvanised into life.

Almost embarrassed to be in each other's company now we all dressed hurriedly. Shame-faced, the men added a considerable amount to the stack of tenners in the chest-of-drawers. They looked 'round quickly to make sure they had all their belongings and we left the little room with its rumpled bed, the room which now reeked—deliciously—of sex.

The others went their way and I followed my friend to his car. We said little on the short drive back to my pitch. He dropped me off there and as I took up my position once again, he leant through the car window and called softly, "All the best, love—that was a night to remember and no mistake!"

I smiled back and gave him a little wave. The truth was that I was now weary of the whole business and much as I'd enjoyed the last couple of hours it was over and I wanted him gone. It had been wonderful—all and more than I could ever have hoped—but it was not the sort of thing that made for a lasting relationship. I smiled to myself as his car pulled away. I was alone on the streets. In all directions empty wet cobbles stretched, reflecting intermittently the orange glare of the sodium lights. The other girls had evidently finished for the night. Surely soon, now, I'd see your car in the distance. You'd come for me and take me home.

Stephen Van Scoyoc
A Friendly Gesture

The sun was just beginning to close on the horizon, casting long shadows of crimson and purple upon the sea, but it didn't look like the sun would beat the heavy clouds that were swiftly rolling in. I wasn't really in a hurry to beat the rain that was sure to come so I leaned back, took another sip of *vino verde tinto*, and lit up a fat Cuban cigar. The smoke curled out lazily into the cooling evening air.

I had just finished a sumptuous meal of *sardinha grelhada*, fresh sardines grilled over a charcoal fire. It was early November and this was the time to be in Alva—after all the tourists had returned to their native countries. The small village once again belonged mostly to the locals and I valued the solitude as much as they.

As I took another long drag of the smooth cigar I was startled by the angry shouts of a woman followed by the crash of a suitcase landing on the pavement across the street. A second case followed close behind with a loud thud. Life on the street stopped and all eyes turned to see an attractive young woman, obviously furious, stalking down the narrow stairs. She turned at the bottom and shouted back up the corridor, shaking her fist. A door slammed loudly and she turned, snatched up the heavy cases, and staggered up the hill precariously in her stilettos away from the cove. She was dressed to party, but it looked like the party was over. Life quickly returned to normal, as though this happened all the time. I watched with fascination and, admittedly, with a bit of lust as the woman disappeared onto one of the many side streets.

A fat raindrop landed on my arm and in seconds more began dropping down with loud pops on the canopy behind me. I scooted my chair back under the shelter, intent on finishing my cigar before starting back for my flat. Everyone else was already scattering into the street and heading for bars, clubs, and home. I knew I would get soaked whether I left right away or waited a few minutes. I took another long drag on the cigar as my waitress smiled at me.

Finally I set the still smouldering stub of my cigar in the tray, slipped a few bills under my wine glass, bid my host *boa noite*, and set off into the gathering dusk and rain. The rain was delightfully cool and I was, of course, soaked through by the time I reached the *centro cidade*. I walked slowly along, enjoying the sensual sensation as the rain plastered my clothes to my body. I turned the corner down a narrow street to cut across to my flat and nearly stumbled over the woman I had seen earlier. Now she was sitting on her suitcases and drenched by the rain. I caught my balance just before falling over on her.

"Desculpe," I said, using one of the few words of Portuguese in my vocabulary.

She looked up at me with eyes that streamed tears and mascara. Stray curls of her nearly black hair clung in ringlets to her wet cheeks. She muttered something to me which I didn't understand.

"Não entendo—fala inglês?" was the only thing I could say and that used up most of the rest of my knowledge of Portuguese.

She shook her head. She spoke no English and I spoke no Portuguese. It was a clumsy few moments. I looked around but the streets were empty. I'm typically a generous person and I wanted to help this young woman. I cleared my throat to get her to look up at me.

"Casa?" I asked while pointing toward the flats I was staying in.

She looked very hesitant, but the rain was falling even harder than before and she nodded her head with reluctance. She stood and I quickly picked up her cases and we began walking toward my flats.

We were both drenched to the core as we stood in the doorway of my modern holiday flat while I fumbled for my keys in the gloomy light. The flat was only a few years old, sheathed in white stucco and surrounded by palms and landscaped flowers. I only came here a few weeks out of the year, during the winter. The rest of the time I rented it out to families for their holidays. I came here to escape—and write.

The door opened and I stepped back to let her in. The sparsely furnished flat was a welcome respite from the intense storm outside. My guest had turned and waited for me. I motioned for her to follow me and took her into an empty bedroom where I set her cases on one of the beds. I pointed across the hallway to the bathroom. She nodded gratefully and I walked out into the kitchen to put a kettle of water on to boil.

I caught her eye as she started for the bathroom with a bundle of clothes in her hands.

"Bica?" I asked.

She stopped and for a moment the tenseness eased from her face.

"Café com leite—faz favor."

"Good," I thought, just the way I like it too.

"Obrigada," I heard her say as she stepped into the bath.

I made the coffee and set her cup on the table where my books and manuscripts were piled beside my notebook computer. I headed for the bathroom in my own room for a shower and dry clothes. When I came out I noticed that the coffee I had left for my guest was gone as was one of my books although I wasn't sure which one. The door to her room was closed but a light glowed softly from beneath the door. I made myself another cup of coffee and, feeling inspired by this woman's beauty and predicament, sat down to write another story for my erotica series. I heard the light click off in her room a couple of hours later and decided to turn in myself.

I woke to the delicious smell of food cooking in the kitchen. I quickly pulled on my running shorts and stepped into the main room. I padded softly across the dark, red clay tiles, my still warm feet leaving steamy footprints on the cool floor. I noticed that her bags were already packed and sitting beside the front door. I peeked around the door to the kitchen and saw my guest, her back to me, as she stirred *ovos* in a pan. A plate of fried *chorizo* and *faimbre* was already sitting on the counter top. My guest was wearing a man's long, white Oxford shirt, one of mine I realised. Her long, wavy, black hair was pinned high upon her head while a few feathery wisps tickled the nape of her neck. Her skin glowed with the dark brown of her Moorish heritage and hours spent in the sun. I made a small noise and stepped into the room. She turned to me with a bright smile.

"Pequeno almoço?"

I wasn't sure what it meant but I nodded my head anyway and watched as she scooped the eggs from the pan onto the waiting plates. I nearly gasped aloud as she turned and I realised the shirt was fastened by only one button and that she was gloriously naked beneath. The brown skin of her breasts teased beneath the cotton fabric and a patch of thick black hair glistened between her legs. I was instantly aware of my cock pressing insistently against my shorts. Before I could avert my stare she noticed me and glanced down at my own crotch with a sly smile and a glimmer in dark eyes. Embarrassed, I quickly turned my eyes toward the food she was dishing up. Although I had found her attractive, it was never my intention to seduce her.

We sat at the table and ate mostly in silence. We shared some sign language as she motioned to the books and computer, wondering if I was a writer. The food was as gorgeous as the woman and, I admit, I stole as many glances at her as I could during our quiet meal. I knew she would be gone soon and I wanted to capture her essence, her spirit. When we finished eating we picked up our large cups of coffee and sat down in the lounge to gaze out into the courtyard of my building. The rain had long gone and the sun shone brilliantly upon the tropical plants and flowers. Birds flitted about from tree to tree and the noise of insects filled the air. I heard the clink of her coffee cup as she set it down on the side table. I swiftly gulped down my last swallow and looked at her. Her expression had changed.

She stood and slowly walked the few steps between us. She looked into my eyes, unbuttoned her shirt, and knelt before me. I felt my cock stirring once again at her unmistakable sensuality. The shirt parted and opened her body to my view. Her breasts were dark and her nipples aroused from the caress of the soft fabric. Her hands slowly trailed up to her head and released the clip that had pinned her luxurious and fragrant hair to her head. She shook her head and her hair gently cascaded down over her shoulders and breasts. Her hands began to softly stroke my cock through the fabric of my shorts. Like most men I always wake with a tremendous erection and I was quick to respond. I hadn't been with a woman in weeks so with her few strokes my desire for her was suddenly insatiable. She tugged my shorts down off my hips, over my legs, and dropped them on the floor beside her.

I sighed and leaned back against the sofa when I realised what she was about to do. My guest lowered her head over my cock, draping her long hair over my thighs and hips, and slowly took my cock into her mouth. Her mouth was still warm from the coffee and I felt myself dissolve into her. She began to bob slowly and rhythmically on my cock while at the same time and with the same rhythm stroked herself. Small muffled sounds of pleasure vibrated around my cock as we both became lost in the sensations.

Slowly she pulled her mouth free and raised her fingers, glistening with her own silky wetness, to my mouth. I eagerly took her fingers into my mouth as she had my cock and savoured the scent of her body and the taste of her desire. Her eyes closed and she purred with a barely audible moan of pleasure.

My guest raised herself up slowly, letting the weight of her breasts trail over my legs, and then straddled me, posing her cunt over my cock. I started to put my hands on her waist, but she pushed them away and pinned them to the sofa. As she leant forward her hair swirled around my face and her nipples teased the skin of my chest. Her cunt swallowed my cock the same way her mouth had, slowly and deliciously. She pulled her hands away from mine and gripped my shoulders as she began to rhythmically thrust herself deeply onto my cock.

I looked into her face and realised that this was no pity fuck. It wasn't even a thank you fuck. It was an angry fuck. This woman was furious with men and to prove it she was going to use me the same way she felt used. I understood perfectly. She didn't want me to touch her. She wanted to take me, please herself, and, I suspected, leave when she was satisfied. I was okay with that.

The rhythm began to speed up as she furiously ground her clit into my body. My cock swelled deep within her and I willed myself to hold back until the right moment. Her fingers dug into my flesh and her moans filled the room and echoed out into the courtyard. Her shoulders bunched up and her neck arched back as she suddenly slowed then stopped grinding. She thrust hard and deep onto me with grunts that were nearly screams before beginning to shudder as her body was racked with an intense orgasm. I could wait no longer and cried out myself as my cum, aching from weeks of celibacy, flowed into her warm cunt. She collapsed forward into me, sobbing, as my cock continued to pulse with rapture. My arms wrapped around her and held her tight as her gasps subsided. Finally, we were silent and unmoving. Her breathing was soft and relaxed in my ear. I thought I heard a knocking at the door.

My guest lifted her head, pulled away the hair from her face, and smiled at me. She gave me a quick kiss on the lips and lifted herself free of me. My cum dribbled down her leg and white drops fell to the floor. Her head turned to the door and shouted out something that I didn't understand. She began buttoning up her shirt, my shirt! She bounced into her room and out again almost as quickly wearing blue jeans and sandals. She stopped as she passed me, gave me another quick kiss, and whispered in my ear "thank you."

I was so stunned I could say nothing and just watched her open the door to a friend nearly as beautiful as her. I heard giggles and the scrape of the cases as the two women dragged them outdoors. The door closed and I could hear them chattering away as they walked through the courtyard. Soon I was in silence again.

I finally gathered up my strength to stand. I looked about the room, almost as if to convince myself she had really been here. I walked into "her" room and inhaled deeply. The air was still fragrant with her scent. My eyes were drawn to a scrap of paper on the bed. I picked it up. It was written in English.

"Thank you for being kind. I enjoy your book. I hope don't mind I took it with me."

I smiled to myself at the realisation that my guest had spoken English after all. I turned the note over and on the back was a name and an address—hers I hoped. I wondered which book she had taken so I went back to the table to examine the books. Only one was missing—*Closet Desire.*

Angela Wallis
Dancing in the Dark

Well I was decked out, that's for sure. The Old Coot couldn't fault me on that. No idea why or where he was dragging me this time, but I am betting I make an impression, wherever it is. I looked like a sexy silverfish, without all the yucky bug legs. A black on silver backless lace teddy from Vic Sec, scoop neckline down to the nips, and sides cut up past my hipbones. Shimmering silver thigh tops that stopped a few inches from the "V" of my teddy. Topped off with silver lame cocktail dress, choker collar, falling down the sides of my breasts, just concealing the teddy, and backless. A hem line that just skimmed the tops of my stockings. And as the finale, six inch silver and black heels, ankle straps, and a sexy crisscross weave of delicate straps over the arch. Bare toes, blood red toe nails. Eighty-five dollar pedicure worth every cent. Next to baby doll faces, the Old Coot had an avid thing for toes. So toes he would get.

By now I wasn't impressed by the limo. I mean Franco the chauffeur took me everywhere. It got old. Although I was definitely impressed with Franco's driving ability—if ya get my drift—but that's another story. So George—yeah , no shit, the Coot's name is George—and me are pulling up to this huge old warehouse thing. Which woulda weirded me out 'cept a line of limo's was letting off a bevy of be-gowned young beauties—all tall, all leggy, all plastic. At least George had the taste to keep a brunette—rich wild hair to my shoulders, child-like eyes, but nothing child-like about the firm round titties, the tight waist, or the flaring hipbones. Along with the bevy of babes was the usual collection of Coots. All looking rich and powerful in evening wear. They might broker power on Wall Street, but my mind kept drifting to wrapping my thighs around where Franco kept his power. The deep-eyed Italian giving me a wink as he holds the door for me. Oh Angela, Angela, don't let your mind go there girl.

Inside was a truly unexpected experience. Dimly lit with drab hallways leading to door after door in what seemed to be a circle. No one spoke. Couples disappearing through the doorways. George escorting me through one and into what was simply a room—hardwood, tasteful wallpaper, and gentle lighting. Music. No chairs. Nothing. Way weird. We stood silent. I got a none to gentle jab in my ribs when I tried to whisper a question to the Old Coot. "Be still Angela!" in his boardroom voice. Waiting.

Then the whole wall lights up and I realize we are looking through a huge one-way mirror into a rather large room—same hardwood floor, brightly lit, and also without a stick of furniture And, standing still as a statue in the middle of the room, the most stunning, scrumptious, muffin of a woman I have ever laid my little lezzie eyes on. Oh my. Exotic. Her hair an unreal shade of red, coifed to perfection, flowing forward to frame her face and then back in a sculpted shape that was a testament to styling gel. Her face with perfect bones and almond eyes, sensuous but nasty lips. Overly made up but beautifully striking.

But then, oh ladies of the Dare, then the gown. Let me tell you about her gown. To kill for—red—run through with a white feather like patter of shimmering silk, a crossing halter top that shaped her breasts, exposing the sides, cut down the front to her belly button, no back, full length and hugging her perfect hips like shining red water, a slit to her hip. Nude stockings with flecks of white like snowflakes. And shoes, man I hadda find out where she shopped for shoes. Red, ridiculous heels, a lattice of straps claiming to hold them on her perfect bare feet. Toes with white polish flecked in red. I knew George was looking at the toes. She was something out of the imagination of some erotic cartoonist. The image of the world's most desirable woman wrought in flesh before us.

Well, to get to the chase. Soon a man is brought into the large room by a human looking woman. He, like the lady in red, is a caricature of the tall svelte male. Black hair swept back, face chiseled and made up, a tall, slim and perfectly proportioned body in a black and silver tuxedo. Dramatic. And blindfolded. So now what is this? I am asking. It's like that damn peep show I sneaked into on a dare back in college, except the grubby booths have been replaced by understated larger rooms— and the fat stripper replaced by human mannequins. Man, the Old Coot Society had outdone themselves.

Then remarkably, a full THX sound system filling the building with an orchestra of music. And they dance. He takes her hand, blindfold and all, as if they had done this a thousand times, and by what seems pure instinct, leads her into an intricate and marvelous dance. Ballroom dancing. A peep show with fucking ballroom dancing. My eyes actually rolled. Take me home, seen it all.

But then George is leaving me! Hands me a blindfold. "Each time you hear a chime," he whispers, "put this on, then remove it when you hear the next chime."

"George!" I hiss, and I think I stamped my red toes. "What is this!"

"Angelica! Don't make me come up there!" Now his Daddy voice and I know not to fuck with that!

So watching the dance. Alone. God they are like swans. Her back perfectly formed like the neck of a swan, from the neck held back to the inward curve above her hips. Her body flowing around her sightless partner. Doing things on heels that made me cry in envy. And him. At once upright and firm yet fluid, and somehow always leading his partner in the dance, as if parting a way for her perfection. Jeez. This was hot.

"Chime"

Blindfolded, dutifully. The door opens, a body enters, not George by the cologne. Not a word. I am taken in skillful arms against a tall male body. Holding me still for a moment as a golfer might pause before an elegant back swing. And then we dance. Yes, in the small room. Somehow quite comfortable, never running headlong into walls. Me actually struggling to keep up, but soon feeling like a partner myself. The hands. Touching softly but boldly, down my bare back, across the taut curve of my cheeks, back up my sides, leading me to pirouette away and back to him. Always his hands told me he was the master of this dance. Hugging each other, my breasts fully pressed against a strong chest. His body warm. My body warm. Breathing more heavily than the exertion would call for.

"Chime"

He is gone when I take off the blindfold. I watch in awe again at the partners in the center floor. Now more closely flowing in circles around the floor. His body always caressing hers. Her long bared leg brushing along his strong legs. Her leg lifted to be held as she bends back incredibly, her face almost to the floor, her leg impossibly long and elegant. His hand free to caress the silk skin over her thigh. White satin panties. Woof! This girl's gotta dress me from now on.

"Chime"

Blindfold. Yet another man enters, smelling only of unscented soap and some simple shampoo. And yes, we dance. The music changing, ascending, soothing, always like the heart beat of the building itself. He bends me back. I do a poor imitation of the perfect female, but the touch of his fingers on my thigh, then, yes, then on my silver panties, just a caress along the V formed between my thighs, enough, just enough to coax my tender bud from its frock. Now its unfolded and damp frock. A dampness with a scent that rose above the slight scent of my warm body. I sensed it in the air and he did too. When we finished he was behind me, his hands coming up my stomach, onto my firm breasts, the thin dress and lace teddy not concealing the hardening spikes of my nipples. He pinches, holds them, extends them gently till the perfect point, the pleasure giving way to pain, release. He is gone.

"Chime"

Alone I cannot keep my fingers from the hem of my skirt, easily slipping under my lace panties. Finding a flood of my girl cum ready to pour from me, onto my eager fingers, now slick from the fountain of my slit, working a finger up inside that wonderful warm place, behind my clitty, my thumb pressing on my bud from above. Teasing and tormenting myself, all the time the couple playing out their sensuous dance, teasing and tormenting each other. Somehow my panties are off, somewhere on the floor. My fingers dancing on my reddened and warm clit.

"Chime"

Ooops. Caught reddened and warm handed—so to speak. My blindfold hurriedly tugged back down. My next mystery partner smiling, not objecting, lifting my hand to his lips, a kiss, then a lingering sucking of my thin, slick fingers. Blood red nails. We dance. But briefly, so briefly, since no one can really dance on their knees right? I mean can any of you? In the dark, wordless room my hand finding a familiar warm pulsing and ever growing Yule log. Whose Yule log I'll never know. But I like the image. He liked the touch of my tongue on the bulbous tip, liked the kisses and licking down the underside 'till his fat, engorged balls filled my mouth. One, the other, both. Much mouth, open wide. Realizing the next chime was imminent I got down to basics. Cocksucking 101. Lips pursed, kissing, tasting the slick early traces of cum, then opening, feeling his hand on my hair, a moan, then my moan, so hot on my tongue with the vein beating menacingly. Well it took awhile, but we got in under the chime. Splat, a gob hits my tonsils, then all the rest, pumping his thick salty semen onto my tongue, puffing my cheeks out, coating my teeth. Him bearing down, soundless but his firm hand leaving no doubt how this was gonna finish up. Big Gulp, like *Seven Eleven.* Mmmmmm, why I like that stuff is still a mystery to me.

"Chime"

So it continued. How long? I could not keep track and I doubt you could have either, ladies. Alternating between watching the mating dance of the swans and the intimate touches of unseen, unknown, strangers. Filling the room, the night, as if my bedroom, with a succession of partners, touching, daring, never extorting but fulfilling themselves—and myself. The erotic and the sexual so intertwined. Where is that line? I think it blurred that night, but I'm willing to go back and try to find it? Angie's always been an eager learner.

"Chime"

Stephen Van Scoyoc
Eclipse

"Roni! What's wrong?"

Sharon was instantly at my side, bending over with me as I doubled up in pain. I couldn't straighten up as the spasm tightened its grip on me. I remember thinking to myself "it isn't time yet." Stars began to shoot through my head as I felt myself falling to the ground. I was aware of Sharon by my side—distant voices—footsteps approaching—the sun burning into my skin—the smell of moist dirt—then I drifted even farther away. I was aware of being half-carried, half-dragged—rough hands on my body—tugging at me—Sharon pleading with them to be careful.

*   *   *

That's how it all started—I should have known then—maybe I wouldn't be here now—facing inevitable doom at the hands of these savages. I look up at the moon—a tiny sliver in the sky just behind my shoulder—shining down on me with that deceitful grin. I should have known. I feel it tugging at me now, at my womb with the force of a full moon, but there she smiles, a thin slice of lunacy, mocking me.

My wrists are on fire where the drying leather thongs have sliced into my flesh. My shoulders ache from my arms being so brutally drawn up behind me. They've taken no chances. My wrists and ankles were bound three days ago with wet leather and each day, in the sun, they have tightened in the scorching sun. I no longer feel the burns on my naked skin except when my hair, caked in mud and my own sweat scratches harshly against me. Wide leather straps, also wet three days ago, encircle me and threaten to crush me as they too dry in the baking sun. They won't let me die like this—they have other, less merciful plans.

*　　　　　　*　　　　　　*

I woke in a hospital or for what passes for one in this brutal land. A small, metal hut built by missionaries a century ago and now taken over by the local tribes. I remembered being taken out of the back of a truck, on a stretcher, and carried into the stench of death and disinfectant. Sharon was there but I couldn't understand what she was saying. Either I was delirious—or she was.

The spasms passed and I opened my eyes. It was dim. The room I was in was filled with the dying in rows of metal-framed beds. I tried to raise myself but found my arms secured at my side to the bed by worn leather restraints. Did they think I was insane? I pondered. Sharon was sleeping in a chair beside the bed. I tried to speak to her, but my voice was silent.

I watched as the doctor began his rounds with a short, dark woman trailing dutifully behind with a tray of instruments and medicines. He was in no hurry as he ambled my way. When he arrived at the foot of my bed Sharon stirred and looked up at him. He felt my head, pressed on my belly, and turned to speak to the nurse behind him. She looked familiar to me, but I don't know why. I'd never been here before. She stepped forward and halted in mid-step, dropping her tray with a deafening clatter. She was looking at me, glaring at me. Her eyes widened and her nostrils flared. I had seen that look before in the eyes of a gazelle as a lioness crushed its throat. It was the face of death. Without a word she turned and fled from the room while the doctor looked on in astonishment.

Sharon talked with the doctor a moment and he soon carried on with his rounds.

"They're just going to watch you for a while," she said, trying to soothe me.

I adored Sharon, loved her with all my heart. We had met when I moved to New York from Romania. We moved in together almost immediately. My name had been Veronika, taken from my grandmother, but Sharon had changed it to Roni. I had chosen her as the one I wanted to spend my eternity with, but she had to choose me. So I waited patiently and enjoyed our time together. This had been her idea. "Have an adventure," she had said. So here we were at a posh resort in Mexico, joining the other throngs of tourists awaiting the total eclipse of the sun—that magical moment when the moon and the sun line up and the darkness of the night races across the face of the Earth.

"Don't worry," she said, "you'll be fine and we'll do just what we planned."

Suddenly it had occurred to me, that was it, the eclipse. That's how the moon had fooled me so easily. I had felt it. The familiar stirring inside my body. The weight building in my belly, the heavy swelling in my breasts, the aching to be filled as my blood began to surge and froth. It had only been two weeks since the blood had flowed, when the tidal tug of the moon had drawn upon me. Now it was worse—far worse. Each day as the moon and sun passed closer and closer to one another, I felt it would tear me apart. Surely the eclipse would kill me. I had heard the legends but in my lust for Sharon, in my obsession to possess her, I had not heard my mother's words warning me. I knew what I needed to do, but I had to get out of here.

"Get me out of here—please," I begged Sharon in a hoarse whisper and gripped her fingers feebly in my own.

"Don't worry—you'll be fine," she reassured me.

"Please," I begged.

The sun was going down, retreating to the other side of Earth with the moon. I felt peace returning to me.

"I'm going back to the hotel to get some things for us—I'll be back first thing in the morning," Sharon said to me.

I panicked and pulled against the restraints. I could see tears welling in Sharon's eyes so I relented, knew it was hopeless. I would have to be patient and wait until morning. I watched Sharon disappear with our tour guide. Seconds later I could hear the rickety old truck rumbling down the dirt path toward the city. I tried to sleep and finally fell into a fitful slumber.

*　　　　　*　　　　　*

I look over my shoulder again toward my mistress, the moon, but she has gone. Tomorrow she will join the sun and together they will draw together and join in the sky, drawing me apart from within. I'm comforted by a moist, cool breeze flowing through the jungle. It must be nearing midnight and it is silent in the village. The jungle is vibrant with life, but here within the village I feel I am the only creature still awake—utterly alone. But I am not alone. I hear the splash of water behind me and know that the boy is watching me again. Keeping his distance always and yet wanting me. I can sense his desire for me. The villagers have been warned to stay away from me, not to look at me, not to touch me. This boy, barely a young man, is drawn to me as I had hoped. That is why they fear me and why I might just yet survive. Each night since I have arrived, while the others have slept, he has brought me water to soothe my lips, to cool my seething blood. I know he will come up behind me silently, not show himself, but I will feel his eyes on me. I will feel the stirring in his loins for me.

*　　　　　*　　　　　*

It was in the night as I slept in that dreadful hospital that they came for me. Stalkers in the night, stealing to my bedside. I awoke to the feeling of rags being stuffed into my mouth, nearly down my throat so that I gagged, and being knotted tightly into place. My gown was being cut from my body with large menacing knives searing the cloth. Rough

· 109 ·

hands pummelled me as other sets of hands tore my hands from the restraints and bound them tightly behind my back. My legs too were bound tightly together. As I was lifted onto a man's broad shoulders I briefly saw that woman again, this time with victory in her eye's—like a lioness taking her kill, only this time it was the prey capturing the predator—as she pulled a thick canvas bag over my face.

I was thrown roughly over the back of an animal, a donkey, and strapped tightly to it. We began moving immediately. I was aware of brushes and rough tree bark scraping against me as we travelled through the night. As daylight approached I could feel the tug in my bowels again and its urgent pain swiftly displaced the discomfort of my aching arms. The sweltering sun began to boil away my sweat as I felt my skin turning raw and blistering in the open sun. Insects swarmed around my wounds, feeding on my flesh and blood. I couldn't scream or struggle or even cry. I struggled to breathe in the bag as it became soaked in my sweat and the tiny pores of the canvas closed, threatening to suffocate me.

Night was fast approaching by the time we reached this hidden village. I could hear the shuffling of feet as the villagers crowded in warily to catch a glimpse of me. The woman who had led in my capture was speaking excitedly. I had never spoken the language but I understood the ancient tongue—knew that I was considered evil—knew that I was to be sacrificed during the eclipse—knew that I was to be burned—alive and screaming in agony.

I was led, like an animal, to an altar near the village's edge. It had been built just for me. I could smell the charcoal that the elders had prepared from decaying trees and the freshly sawn lumber. I could also smell the modern day influence of petrol. They were taking no chances with me. Jagged splinters thrust sharply into my knees as I was forced down onto the altar. Wet thongs of animal hide were stretched around my wrists and ankles, twisted with a stick like a tourniquet, and securely tied into place. Wider thongs were stretched over my body, cinching my waist and crushing my swollen breasts. I was too weary, too resigned to protest. Finally a leather thong was passed around my throat and secured to a pillar in the centre of the altar. The bag was removed and as I blinked away the bright, evening sun I saw the villagers as eerie shadows, wearing little more than leather loin-cloths over their mud-caked, bronzed skin, staring at me in hatred. They were brandishing sticks and rocks as a village elder chanted incoherently before me. When he stepped away I felt a barrage of stones pelting my body followed by the sharp sting of branches whipping my skin. The women stood back and hurled stones or spit at me. The men wielded thick branches which landed with a thud upon my body. The worst were the children who dashed in like tiny predators to strike viciously with thin branches before dashing away like mongooses tormenting a snake. My mind was soon dulled by the pain and I endured it without a whimper.

*　　　　　*　　　　　*

I have knelt here now for three days, beyond hope of rescue, waiting for my ultimate death. The pain in my womb is growing stronger although it is still on that precipice between unendurable pain and exquisite ecstasy. The hunger that drives me is gnawing at me, replacing my resignation with hope.

I am startled by the gourd being pressed to my lips and the smell of stagnant water as it flows over my lips. I lap hungrily at the life giving fluid, choking as it burns my cracked throat. I can feel him behind me this time, closer than before, the warmth of his body, the smell of him, a man about to be born. His skin, warm and moist, brushes against mine and I will myself not to flinch. A finger brushes over my nipple. Although chafed by the leather binding it I cannot help responding to the tentative touch. The fire spreads through my breast and the nipple hardens beneath his rough fingertip. Encouraged, his warm hand takes its fill of my swollen flesh and a soft moan escapes from my lips as I close my eyes and focus upon his touch, trying to draw him in as my own hunger grows.

I can sense him swelling with desire, wanting me, needing me. I know that he is close enough now. My musky scent fills his nostrils, its tendrils touch his brain deeply, and arouses the primitive drives that will save me. My body opens and my lips swell with the blood surging within me. He looks around carefully before gliding before me. His skin glistens in the reflected firelight and he rises before me, facing me. My mouth opens and takes him deeply. I can feel him growing and as his strength fills my mouth I can also feel weakness sweeping the rest of his body. Each time I feel that sweet drop of life form on his tip I retreat slightly and savour it, fuelling his hunger for me. He pulls away from me and I can feel that he is a man now, controlled by his own hunger and not by the village elders.

He looks into my eyes, still wary of me, but overcome by his desire for me. I must be the ultimate prize, the evil woman who frightens his people. He will be legendary if he can conquer me, dominate me, control me. To survive, I will let him—for now.

A bright blade flashes in the darkness and flies toward my flesh. I feel the animal sinews binding my ankles draw away as my blood screams through my veins to fill the void. My arms are still tightly bound behind me, but I am balanced lightly on my toes now, crouching before him, his supplicant. He sits before me, his erection rising high into the night. I creep forward, astride him, and settle myself onto him, eagerly swallowing him into my depths. I try to control my hunger, resist the temptation to devour him in one brilliant flash of consumption.

I feel satisfaction as his eyes roll back and close. I lower myself further and feel him pressing against my womb, countering the effects of the moon, the sun, and my past. He stretches me, fills me, feeds my hunger. I am ravenous and voracious as I feel his strength swelling within me. He lies back against my altar of sacrifice and I am free to feed upon his flesh. I taste that first drop of his life, a tiny glowing pearl, within me and I must have the rest. The quickening approaches and I must have it all. I begin to feed and his life rushes forth, filling me. The blood begins to flow as he jerks beneath me. Each convulsion fills me with his life, nurtures me, and drains him.

A black pool of life, thick and viscous, gathers around us upon the altar. He is ebbing away before me as I feel my strength return. My hands and arms flow like liquid out of their bonds and I lean forward to suck the last drops of life from his quieting body. I rest my hands heavily upon his chest as bright lights fill my eyes and my body shudders in rapture. He is motionless beneath me, a boy once again, an innocent sacrifice, as I pull free of him and spring upon the soft, yielding Earth of the jungle floor.

My mistress is beginning to slip above the horizon and dim crimson light kisses the Earth as she and the sun tug one another. Quietly I lift one of the metal cans and pour the pungent petrol over the breathless body. It mixes with our blood, flows into the porous wood of my altar, and trickles onto the Earth. Shielding my eyes from the fire I take a glowing stick and fling it at my altar. A shower of sparks erupts and ignites the vapours. I am already running into the welcoming depths of darkness when the altar explodes behind me. I see my black shadow cast on the ground before me, etched in the white light which will blind the villagers and cloak me in darkness. The roar of the flames is distant when I hear the first wails rise from the village as the would be lioness discovers her dead cub. I am the powerful predator once more.

I am running steadily now, loping gracefully through the under-growth. I know my destination back to Sharon. Sharon is different from the boy. She must give herself to me willingly. I will not take all of her—only just enough—and she will join me for eternity—during the eclipse.

Susan Van Scoyoc
Jane and Merlin

Desperate to save the nation Jane embraced this adventure just as she had many others during Britain's darkest hour. As she approached the gold mine used to supply the royal wedding rings Jane hoped this was at last the right location to find Merlin. She had searched the caverns and castles of Wales but now those clever chaps from Whitehall had sent a message telling her to get straight to Cornwall.

Jane started to descend the rickety ladder down into he depths of the mine. No lifts here.

"Damn," Jane muttered as her uniform button caught on one of the protruding rocks. A few moments later, "damn" again as her uniform jacket was snagged once more and instead of the pristine military uniform Jane was now clothed in a jacket with buttons loose and undone with her blouse ruffled and breasts clearly swelling beneath. This was the disheveled picture she presented to the generals and intelligence chaps, already gathered at the base of the mine shaft. Jane was conscious of her torn clothing but the generals, all middle aged men seemed to be more interested than disapproving.

As Jane made her way through the mine to the location given to her by those intelligence chappies she found more and more of her uniform tattered and torn by the inhospitable surroundings.

Finally she reached the entrance to the hidden section of the mine, the clearing ready for her entry. The miners, patriots all, had been sworn to secrecy over what they had found. As Cornish men, even above their British nationality, they had a pride and reliability that the British agents knew they could trust.

Jane surveyed the scene. An elderly but distinguished man lay on a golden slab as if he were sleeping. Only the inscriptions on the slab revealed the identity of the sleeper—Merlin, magician, teacher and friend to Arthur and Guinevere.

Jane had asked to be alone because she knew that what came next was not for the public eye. She had to seduce Merlin into the present and she wondered how to start. How would a man who has slept for hundreds of years like to be wakened?

Jane stepped forward, knelt down at the foot of the slab and lent forward pulling aside Merlin's lose flowing robes as she did so. With a strong, slow intake of breath Jane reminded herself *For king and country* as she lowered her full lips over the slumbering cock and started to suck. Gently at first Jane sucked and licked, wondering if she was wasting her time. But just as she was about to release this sleeping male member from her mouth she felt the cock give a small jerk. Jane knew what to do. She started to slurp and suck, putting true British backbone into her efforts until she felt the cock grow to an amazing stiffness. Jane eased off for a moment to observe Merlin—yes his eyes were closed still but his body was stirring along with his cock. Good, she would awake him this way and he would save Britain from a fate worse than death. Jane returned to the task, or should I say cock, in hand. She held this now swollen, eager cock in her fingers whilst taking as much as she could into her mouth. Her slurps and licks changed slowly but surely into the slow rhythmic suck she knew men liked. Surely this Merlin was no different. Certainly so far this ancient magician responded like a man, even if he had slept now for centuries. Jane's head kept bobbing up and down to meet with the growing thrust of this hungry cock.

Jane had been chosen for this mission because of her "experience" so when she felt Merlin ready to come she prepared herself to pull her head away. But at just that moment Merlin groaned loudly and Jane nearly jumped out of her uniform when she felt the strong thrust of Merlin's cock into the back of her throat and his hands holding her head just where he wanted it. Merlin came with the force of a man who has not had sex for centuries. Jane's mouth filled with his cum, her mouth ached and her lips were filled with the final thrusts of the magician as he awoke.

As Merlin released her Jane sat herself up, the copious amounts of cum dribbling from her lips onto her jacket and skirt, leaving white rivulets of cum over her chin and clothes. Merlin looked around him and then directly at Jane.

"Well," he chuckled, "so they sent someone to awake me once more. What do they want this time?"

Jane wiped her mouth on her sleeve and tried to explain about the Germans, the war, the Japanese, the brave few still defending the British shores but her words seemed to fall on deaf ears. Finally Jane explained that Britain needed Merlin's magical powers to help defend their land.

"But I am not yet strong enough my dear," Merlin replied after a moments thought. "I need to be restored to my full power before I can help your land again." Merlin reached over and pressed his hand against Jane's full breast. "You are a beautiful woman—they chose well. What is your name?"

"Jane," she replied, looking down at the state of her uniform now covered with drying cum stains. Jane felt hot and bothered deep in this suffocating mine and slipped out of her jacket and skirt, keeping her white starched shirt on over her camisole, French knickers and stockings.

"Jane," echoed Merlin. "I would rather call you Guinevere. You know Arthur and I shared more than just adventures, we shared our Queen too." Merlin reached again for Jane and started to gently caress her breast. His hands traced the lines of her body and Jane could see his cock becoming firm again already. *Well he is a magician*, she thought to herself, *and my country needs me,* as she allowed the pleasure of those touches to melt her into Merlin's waiting arms. He undid her buttons and traced his fingers over the silky surrounding of her body. He pulled her to him and rolled himself over her. Jane felt herself be taken by this magician, who seemed to be becoming stronger and younger by the minute. Jane felt her French knickers slip from her body and Merlin's cock slip deep into her. She shuddered as she felt the thickness of it stretch and fill her. Jane shuddered as Merlin fixed his own lips firmly over her nipple and suck as she had sucked him. Jane felt the rhythm building as Merlin filled her deep inside. Jane felt her own orgasm approaching as she heard Merlin say over and over with each thrust "Guinevere, Guinevere."

Jane and Merlin lay together for a few minutes in that deep, calm silence that follows intense love-making. Jane felt deeply satisfied and it took her time to come back to the mission in hand. But her country needed her to act and act fast. "Merlin, I was sent here by my government to ask you to save our country. I need your help. We need your help."

Merlin sat and surveyed this English beauty barely covered in tatters, her swollen lips, her face and feminine body both swollen and red from pleasure.

"I am willing to help you and your country again as I did in the past. I am willing but still unable. I need more from you Guinevere. I need something from you that you have never shared with another man. I need your virginity."

Jane's head reeled. What was this strange magician talking about and why, each time he came inside her did he seem to become stronger and younger. There was no understanding this except to say it was magic. Virginity? Jane had not been a virgin for years now. The Secret Service used her for her sensual and sexual charms. Mati Hari had nothing on Jane. What could this magician mean?

Jane felt his arm grasp her waist and his other hand reach down to stroke her swollen lips. She was wet from the mingling of their juices and his fingers probed her body just as his cock had minutes before.

This magician knew how to arouse her and soon Jane was arching her back and submitting to the waves of pleasure pulsing through her cunt. She thrust back onto his finger and it pressed deeper and deeper. She thrust more and suddenly felt a burning, intense pleasure-pain rack her body as Merlin thrust another finger into her arse. Before Jane could react Merlin shifted his weight and the arm which had held her tight flipped her over so her backside was exposed to his gaze. Jane felt Merlin's cock stroke her arse gently and teasingly. She couldn't decide whether it was pleasurable or not. This was not anything she had done before. And then it struck her. This was her virginity. This is what Merlin had meant—somewhere no other man had touched her!

"Ah, Guinevere, you are so beautiful and you have been so free with your favours. But this—this is mine." Jane closed her eyes tight as she felt the head of Merlin's firm cock press at this most tight opening. Jane held herself closed, resisting his entry. But then she remembered *For King and country* so she breathed deep and long, willing herself to relax and even to push back gently against the insistent magician. As he entered her she screamed, but not from pain. Her arse felt as if it was burning and yet the pleasure was intense. Jane tensed and immediately the pleasure left her. "Relax, my Queen, relax and it will be exquisite," Merlin murmured to her. Jane breathed deeply and again felt the intense burning pleasure wash over her, through her. Merlin pushed slowly but firmly deeper into her until Jane wondered how much more she could stand and then he started to rock, gently back and forth pulling her with his movements, moving her with him. He still held her firmly round the waist with one arm, locking their bodies together. His other arm reached down and pressed onto her clit gently then firmly with each rock of their bodies. Jane had never felt intensity such as this. Her body no longer knew where she was filled, cunt or arse, only that she was filled with this man, this magician and that she was racked with orgasm after orgasm. Each gentle rocking of their bodies sent another wave through her until she was screaming the deep guttural cries of an animal. Merlin too joined her cries and the gentle rock became rougher and more intense until he could hold out no longer and filled her once more with his thick cum.

They lay in each others arms, locked together in a lovers' embrace. Jane no longer had any thoughts of her own. She no longer wanted anything except to be with this magician. This is what she had been searching for with her lovers. The screaming intensity. The loss of all sense of who she was or what was being done to her body except that it was good.

It was Merlin who disturbed her blankness this time. "You want me to save your country. I will do so gladly and now, finally I am strong enough. But I want something from you, my dear Guinevere. I want you to be my Queen, to stay by my side and to give yourself to me as you have given yourself to me this day."

Jane stood unsteadily on her feet, her mouth, her cunt and now her arse all showing signs of Merlin's thick copious cum.

"Yes, Merlin, Yes. I will stay with you. I must take you to the generals waiting at the foot of the mine shaft but like this…," Jane nodded to her physical appearance. In an instant Merlin pointed his finger, the same one which had been so deep inside her body and did a different magic—Jane was transformed into Guinevere, a picture from a fantasy-legend.

Stephen Van Scoyoc
Illegal Aliens

Scott Franklin—a normal sort of a fellow with a job in the city, an apartment in the suburbs, and a girlfriend in another town—has an extraordinary experience that he can't deal with on his own. That's what brings him to the office of Dr. Barbara Venable—a specialist in problems of the mind. She leads him into her dimly lit office and settles him into a soft, leather sofa. Opening a note pad, she sits just out of his eyesight and crosses her long, slender legs. Looking up she speaks. What happens next can only happen to those who find themselves trapped—trapped in the erogenous zone.

"Are you ready to begin?"

"Yeah, I 'spose so."

"Tell me about your dream."

"It was no dream—it was real—as real as you and me sitting here."

"Okay—tell me about it."

"It was last Thursday. I was driving over to my girlfriend's house— she lives about twenty miles away—and it was dark and raining buckets. I was late and I hadn't seen her in two weeks so I was driving really fast—too fast—and the wipers weren't working very well. Anyway, I came around a curve and there were really bright lights shining back at me. I knew I was dead—figured I was about to hit somebody head on— felt the car start to slide off the road. The last thing I remembered was the car flipping over in the air and the feeling that I was falling…"

"Did you wreck your car?"

"No—I mean—yes—sort of. I'm not sure. I'll tell you later—it isn't important anyway."

"Okay—go on."

"I must have passed out or something because when I came to I was on a bed or gurney of some kind. I was confused. I thought I was in a hospital, but it was too weird. I couldn't see any people or hear any voices. I could hear humming in the distance, but I couldn't really see anything. I tried to sit up but it was as though I was glued to the mattress. I could slide my body real slowly around on the bed, but I couldn't lift any part of my body from the bed. It was like—like—a magnet was holding me down. I tried to relax and just wait to see what would happen next."

"You're getting very agitated. Now, I want you to close your eyes, clear your mind, and slowly try to recall everything."

"Okay—I'm okay now. I was naked, but it was warm. Not too hot, not too cold, just exactly right. The bed was warm too and moulded itself to me like a gel. I tried to decide if I was injured and where, but I couldn't feel any pain. It just got more and more confusing. When I held my breath I could hear movement—like feet shuffling around—but I couldn't see anyone—not at first anyway."

"How long were you like that?"

"Mmmm—I don't know exactly—an hour maybe?"

"What did you do while you were lying there?"

"I kept trying to stare out into the distance. It was like I was in a room without walls and everything stopped just a few feet away from my bed. No matter how I looked I couldn't see very far. There was light shining on me, but it wasn't very bright—not bright enough to blind me. In fact it was kind of dim. Out of the side of my eyes I could see motion—forms that seemed to shimmer just a little bit, but I could see right through them. I remember thinking it was like some futuristic camouflage. They were mostly gathered around my head, just above my sight. I thought I could feel prodding and touching on my head, but I wasn't sure. I started to think I was crazy—or that I was awake in an operating room—or that I was dead."

"Were you in the hospital by this time?"

"No—just wait—I'm getting there."

"Suddenly I heard voices—some that I hadn't heard for years. It was sort of like a dream, but it wasn't a dream. Then I started to get visions—flashes of people I'd known or places I'd been. They were only there for a fraction of a second. Then there were the smells—my mother's cooking, wet grass—that sort of thing. I began to think I really was dead—you know—my life flashing before my eyes and all that—and that's when things really started to happen."

"What happened?"

"Suddenly I was back in my car—or rather—I was back in the car I had when I was in college. I was in the driver's seat, reclined back and—I wasn't alone."

"Who was with you?"

"Jennifer—my girlfriend—I mean the girlfriend I had then."

"What was she doing there?"

"Ummmm—she was giving me a blowjob. Her head was in my lap and my hand was on her head. I could smell her flowery perfume. I could feel her soft, blonde hair as she bobbed up and down on my cock—we used to do that—make out in the car. It was so incredible, the way she was making me feel. Her mouth was wet and warm and silky around my swollen cock. Her breasts were pressed against my leg and my other hand was stroking the valley of her waist. That's when I realized it wasn't her giving me head—I mean it looked like her and she always felt wonderful, but women—well—women all do it differently and this definitely wasn't Jennifer. It started to feel more and more like the prostitute I had paid in Livorno, Italy—when I was in the Navy—I was so horny from being at sea so long. She started literally fucking my cock with her mouth, trying to make me cum fast and hard. God—I did too—in no time at all. My whole body tensed up, my vision went black, and I came so hard I thought I would pass out."

"When I opened my eyes, I was back in the room, on the bed, held down as before. I remember thinking I must have made quite a mess and that somebody would have to clean me up, but I didn't feel any cum drying on my body. In fact, I could still feel my cock laying heavy and limp on my leg. It wasn't even a little hard. I twitched it a little bit, but it wasn't wet either. That's when it happened again."

"What happened again."

"I was in a room, a big room. It was one of those luxurious mansions like what you see in Miami. The windows were open and there was a breeze blowing through light green, sheer curtains. Through the windows I could see blades of palm leaves swaying in the air. I could smell the sea and hear the waves crashing on the beach. The floor was polished black marble, thickly veined, with plush carpet rugs and a huge bed in the middle of the room. A hand touched my back and I turned around to see the most gorgeous woman I have ever seen—well—I had seen her before—kind of."

"What do you mean?"

"Ummm—sometimes I look at pictures on the web—you know—porn. I remembered being completely taken by this dark-skinned woman with nearly black eyes and dark, flowing hair. She was with a man, but I don't remember what he looked like—didn't actually care at the time. Her body was stunning—I mean perfect in every way. She pushed all the right buttons for me. I got a hard on just looking at her. When I watched her sucking on this man's cock and then fucking him it was almost enough to make me come in my pants."

"Was the man there too?"

"Was the man where? What the fuck are you talking about?"

"Calm down—I mean in the room—was the man there?"

"Oh—no. It was just the two of us. God, she was naked and then I realized that I was too. She knelt down before me, on the thick carpeting, and began to suck my cock just like she did the guy in the web photos. I felt like I hadn't been with a woman in years and almost right away I was ready to cum in her mouth. I wanted to hold back—make things last—but she was having none of it. I heard her starting to moan and that tripped me man—I came in a flood and doubled up over her. She didn't stop and I had to push her away before I fell flat on the floor. She was giggling and smiling at me seductively."

"What happened next? Were you back in this dark room?"

"Oh man—no way—that's when the really bizarre stuff happened. I looked down at my cock and it was hard again—harder than I can ever remember it being. The woman was on the bed, kneeling, with her hand buried between her legs and her head thrown back and lovely breasts thrust forward. She was masturbating and coming in wave after wave of intense pleasure. I felt like an animal—a predator. I wanted her fiercely—I wanted to possess her—mark her as mine—so I pushed her back onto the soft bed and slipped my cock into her body. It felt like we belonged together—the fit was so perfect. I could feel her start cumming around me almost instantly. She reached up and clung to me, drawing me deeper into her body. Her breasts were pressed tight against my chest and her hips were flared wide, her feet pinning me to her cunt. She was so open to me—as though she had completely surrendered. Her breath was hot in my ear. My orgasm exploded and I came even harder this time, filling her with my cum. The scent of my cum mixed with her sex and filled the room with vapours."

"So then you were back in the dark room again?"

"Nope. She was still panting when she pressed her lips to me, drove her tongue down my throat, and turned me over without me ever slipping out of her. I couldn't believe it. My cock was still rock hard and—just like before—I wanted her more than I ever wanted any woman. She started to fuck me—first with long deep strokes—rising up and down over my cock and then—taking me all the way in—grinding hard against me. Her hands were all over her brown body, stroking her smooth, full breasts, pinching her aroused nipples, and caressing her graceful neck. The image was so intense that I could feel the biggest orgasm approaching like a speeding train. She was crouched over me like a cat, ready to spring, growling and snarling, nails digging into my chest. She started to scream. I started to scream. Everything grew dark and my whole being was focused on my cock in her cunt and the sight of her lost in ecstasy. My balls clenched and my cock started to…"

"Time's up! We'll pick up here next time."

"WHAT!? You've got to be fucking kidding! It hasn't even been an hour."

"It's a fifty-minute hour—it's therapeutic."

"What sort of fucking idiot are you—a fifty minute hour—an hour's sixty minutes you quack! Fuck you—I'm not coming back!"

A thoroughly pissed off Scott Franklin storms from Dr. Barbara Venable's office. Cursing that nobody believes him he starts out the door into the parking lot and stops abruptly. Dozens of shimmering forms disappear into the bushes and behind the cars blazing in the summer sun. Scott knows what to look for now and he sees them everywhere. He looks to the sky and warily makes his way to the bus stop. Dr. Venable watches him leave without too much concern—she's seen crazy people before. She closes the door behind him—and locks it.

Angela Wallis

Busted Date

"That rag tag sorry excuse for a boyfriend!"

Seething as I flipped my phone closed and barked at the bartender: "Long Island Tea and now please." Here I am, in my flouncy silk dress. The cleavage is working. The hem line almost illegal. Hair tossed up wild and alluring. Alone. And that son-of-a-bitch thinks he's gonna fuck some tramp and then come to my bed with her stinky pussy smeared all over him? Look up "loser" in the dictionary and see a picture of him. Gawd Angela why has this dragged on for even a year? If you were this wimpy at work you'd be gone in a minute.

But the worst. The worst. Angie hasn't gotten laid since forever and dressing up and looking forward to tonight has got the engines at a full rev. And they don't feel like they're coolin' down. The nips are spiked and the panties are damp. And now what?

The bartender returns with my drink saying: "It was paid for by those guys," pointing to a table with three men in their forties. "Oh blow this off," I'm thinking, "the boyfriend trashes my night and now I'm getting hammered by conventioneers." But why not, they look respectable, go say "thanks" and then it's a hot tub and a bottle of champagne. Alone.

I go over to the table to thank them and they offer me a seat. Against my better judgment I slide onto the empty chair, crossing the legs up high, showing lots of smooth thigh for them to ogle. Which they do. And then outta the blue the oldest says: "Would five hundred cover the three of us for the night?"

I thought I actually heard: "would fire hurt cuddling that tree on the right?" and had no clue what that was about. But then it sunk in. I handle a lot of crap at work so I've developed a poker face. I don't think my face even flinched. They were propositioning me. They thought I was a hotel call girl. A whore. Thinking all of this in a heartbeat, face smooth as glass.

"You're out of your mind aren't you?" saying it matter-of-fact. "We might be able to start talking at five hundred a head—pause—but once you get a taste, you ain't gonna wanna stop at what that will get you."

Soft. Not mean. Not bragging. Just letting them look at the twelve year face and the deep baby doll eyes. Letting 'em take a long look at the body that no way went with the face. And lettin' 'em imagine just what this might be worth. They are slow to come back. I size it up. Forties maybe fifty. I see one Piaget, one Rolex. The older one in a Brooks Brothers suit and one with Cole Hahn loafers. Wedding bands all the way around. Money—established—a lot to lose by fucking around. They must really like the package Angie.

"Maybe we should discuss this somewhere else," the older one suggests.

"Mmmm—I promise you no way anyone's gonna bother us here." I am firm. I'll be at the bar drinking your Long Island Tea (which I just learned has no tea in it? Whaz that?). "Lemme know what the deal is."

Probably close fucking million dollar deals every week and won't pony up for some poor working girl. Sipping my drink, thinking, Angela, you done some stupid shit, but this may take the cake. Are you really gonna? Why not juss fuck em? Get back at the weasel.

Naw, the money's gonna be half the fun.

Wow, I drank that fast!

"One more Sam!" I bark. "On their tab."

Here they come, all of them.

"You know," he says, condescending, "we don't do this sort a thing. Just thought it might be a kick tonight. So give us a general idea what fifteen hundred gets us?"

"Five each? Tell ya exactly big guy. I suck your dicks, you cum in my pretty mouth, and I swallow it. All the way around. The others can watch, whatever. Then you got my best well wishes as ya get outta the room so somebody with some class can get in."

Not liking that.

"Ok, this is silly, we want some fun, and here you are. So at what level do we start having some serious fun, Miss…Miss?"

"Angie, Angela Kowolski," putting my hand out to shake his. Which they all do. Oh God, old white men. What a treat. Me putting two of their hands on my long bare thigh, hoping they can see right down the dress to the nippies.

Serious fun? Like, Angie, bend over and touch your toes serious?

That and whatever. He's burning, wants to fight me or fuck me.

"*Whatever* is ten for the night, out by dawn so I can get a nap before check out. And you pay for the room. And the champagne."

"You are kidding right?"

Bang, I am half way across the lobby before he can catch me. And suddenly we are a happy little party going up to suite 625 in the elevator. Me huggin', rubbing, purring like a happy sex kitten. Oh, after a stop at the *American Express* desk. Amazing the service they provide those Blue or Gold cards or whatever. All hundreds, crisp, one hundred of them in my purse.

In the room they are trying to bolt outta the gate. Jeez the clock ticking and they want their money's worth. But we do the champagne, the intro's, the getting comfy part. Strawberries are great here. Room service guy gives me a wink and I slip him a hundred. What the hell, he needs it right? "Have fun," he whispers, both of us stifling a laugh.

Back in the main room (jeez that weasel missed out on this place) they are shucking ties and coats.

That's when my dress hits the floor. One simple shrug and—poof!—me in my cute little white thong. And then they all look happy. "This is gonna be worth it," the older one says. Coming up to me, arms around, he's big, tall, even in my plats. Hands feeling nice, down on my bare cheeks. God bless the stairstepper. Tilts my head back and puts his lips on mine as if he expects a fight. Nice long, and yes, wet, tongue lashing kiss. I hear a chuckle and see a rubbing of hands from his buds. Ruff, ruff, the wolves smelled a kill.

"I thought whores didn't kiss on the mouth," grins.

I guess I must not be a whore? Innocent.

But now it's time to deal with this situation I've created. Backing up. Hey guys? I know I'm the one who's here to please? But damn I got this bitchin' problem?

"Yes Angie?"

"MY weasel boyfriend has left me high and dry for a month. I'm dying guys. I need some satisfaction. Wow, can't tall ya how much more relaxed and more fun I'd be if I get the juices flowing and have some O's?"

"So whats this deal Angie?" Him picking up champagne. Likes being in control.

"Pay ya each a hunnerd if ya all eat my pussy? Kinda, turn around fair play?"

"A whore wants to pay us to eat pussy?"

This throws him.

"Hey wants a girl to do? So busy working she ain't got time for her-self. You being three fantastically attractive men? What better chance she gonna get?"

Pleading with him. Him smiling. All of them.

"We get the cash upfront? Turn around and all?"

So I walk around the room, handing out hundred dollar bills. Like they gave a shit about the money. Just loved the power thing. Getting back at the whore. Then I stand back and do the real McCoy deal with taking the panties off. Shit they should get sumpin for their money. Hook my thumbs and start 'em down, knees locked, bending at the waist in my six inch heels, slow and putting the ass up high and proud of it. Balancing on one foot to get the panties off (guys? don't try this at home) then the other and then they are much lovin' the bald pussy look. Like a lil' girl.

So I settled back in a soft chair. Spread my white thighs and presented them with my pink, glistening pussy mounds. They were awkward about the whole three guys thing, but they got over it. Champagne, pussy, a pretty girl. So the older one dives in first. And good, really good. The hands on my inner thighs, pushing out, then sliding up to my titties. Nips now seriously red and nailed. His tongue tasting what was about to be a girl cum flood. Did somethin' was new to me. Hands come back down, tongue on my clitty. Both forefingers in my slit, not deep, gentle, but spreads my mounds. "Mmmmmm," then the tongue slips down and up. Oh my. Well that went on for a while until Angie made a huge terrible stain on that really nice upholstered chair. Major cum puddle. Bless him.

He actually said "next." Oh God. So the Cole Hahn guy dived in. So ladies of Litty? This was like a new thing to me. But ya know how they say if ya just drink one wine one day and another the next, ya can't tell the diff? But if you drink them one right after another, you can. This was like that. Three guys in a row in the wonderful world of muff. Each different. Me getting serious mind blow about now. Wondering if things were slipping out of control. This guy a straight muff diver. Ya know, just burrowed in, nose getting wet in there, tongue as far up as ya could hope. Hands on my ass, diggin' in hard. In its way it was super, but actually I thought I was gonna come up short. Which is not the end of the world, but when I am close, wow, there he goes, back there with a finger so fast and unexpected and it was wet and knew what it wanted and Angie had his finger up her tight asshole and was adding to that stain in a major way.

Last guy put my legs up over his shoulders. And by now he's dealing with Niagara Falls down there. But wow he is a pussy slurper. And good. A real mess, the sloppy embarrassing sounds, the gushing. I feel it dripping down my slit, between my cheeks, over my lil rear hole. And staining the fucking chair. Maybe I'm a little vague by now ok? But he lapped it up, liked one hand on my titty and one underneath on my ass or with a finger giving me a little fucking. Pushing that finger in enough to make my hips jerk, squirm on his mouth, his teeth threatening the clitty place. Yikes. But he did it, he bit it, hard, but less than biting it off. I think I screamed. Or evoked dangerous druid spirits. Not sure. But again, the chair took a beating.

So they popped my cork three times in like an hour. Not bad. Whoa, way not bad. So you guys may not wanna read the rest of this. It's kinda ugly but you wanted the truth. And ask me why I did it? I could blame the weasel, frustration, my period starting two days later, but no. I did it cause I could. So sue me.

Since I had splashed my champagne all over their faces, I think they thought it was time to splash theirs all over my face. Or somewhere. But as they huddled to synchronize their attack or whatever, I went to my purse and pulled out a slim black wallet. Walked over to them, bare ass and tits bright pink, dripping cream down my thighs, and showed them a very official looking ID card with a rather nice picture of myself on it. And the words, Angela Kowolski, Special Agent, Federal Bureau of Investigation. Oh the look on their faces.

"I think you guys are gonna wanna be putting your pants on now," I say like reading them Miranda. And they did, and we parted friends—well maybe not—and I am sure ya'll hate me. But the next morning the room service guy brought juice and croissants, unbidden by me, and asked if I might be coming back.

"Sure, my baby smile, why not."

Now what he and I did 'till check out time? Not part of the dare is it?

Stephen Van Scoyoc
Ravished in the Park

Some women are so naive. They don't think men notice what they look like, how desirable they are. This woman was the same way. I saw her in *Next*, looking at clothes for young women even though she certainly wasn't a young woman—thirty-five maybe. I usually hang out there to watch the teenage girls sorting through the sale racks, pressing outfits against their youthful bodies, checking out their shapes. The woman caught my attention because she was small, like the teens, but with that womanly fullness in her curves. She was slender and petite, tiny even. I was attracted first to her breasts—they're my favourite—and hers were on full display. She was wearing a clingy olive coloured cotton top with a deep neckline. The creamy flesh of her breasts pressed tight to the fabric with a liquid fullness. Her khaki trousers were snugly fitted to her small waist and trim hips and cinched up with a dark leather belt. I watched how she moved so gracefully, unaware that I was watching her. I felt my cock getting hard when she brushed her hands over the smooth fullness of her breasts as she fitted tops to herself and glanced in the mirror. I moved closer.

The woman gathered up her choices and turned to brush past me as she headed for the till to make her purchase. I deliberately crowded her and felt the delicious warmth of her breasts graze my arm and across my chest. Sure that nobody was watching me I followed her with my eyes and saw her nipples swollen against the fabric. I turned away, afraid someone might notice that my cock was now fully erect. I willed myself to relax and subtly shifted my cock so it wouldn't be so obvious.

I followed the woman to the till and stood near her as she checked out. The counter help probably thought I was her husband and paid me no attention. When she opened her wallet I could make out her drivers license and made a quick note of her address. It was near the town centre—she had probably walked into town—I might get to follow her home. I decided to leave the shop and wait outside for her. I didn't want her becoming suspicious.

I was well-hidden in the crowd of the high street when I saw her bound out of the shop with a playful lightness usually seen only in young girls. I followed her discretely, well-aware that the CCTV was watching. I knew her address and if she was headed home I wouldn't have any trouble keeping with her. She glanced at her watch and seemed to hesitate a moment before starting out of the town centre—toward her address! The crowd dropped off as we left the precinct and walked toward the residential neighbourhood. Sure enough, she turned down her street, turned up to a new house and disappeared inside. Parked in the drive was a late-model Mercedes. I always liked my women with a little money.

I walked on past her house and circled back into town to collect my car. My plan was to keep an eye on her house and find out what her daily schedule was. Over the years I've learned to be very careful about the women I want—I can't afford to take any chances at getting caught so I don't hang around, letting myself be seen. When I take a woman it's a complete surprise to her. I really wanted this woman so and I knew she would be worth the wait.

Over the coming days—and nights—I drove past her house. When it was dark I would park my car alongside all the others on her street, mingling with the pub crowd down the street. On the fourth night, as I sat drinking an ale in the cooling evening air, I saw her emerge from her house in running clothes. It was nearly 10.00 pm and already there was a slight but steady stream of foot traffic along the road which I could blend into. I swallowed down the last of my ale and set off after her. She walked briskly but hadn't started running yet. I sauntered along after her until she turned into the public park. Excellent, I thought to myself. The park was secluded and large with no roads and very few people this time of year—maybe a few drunks on their way home from the pub. I walked on past the entrance she had disappeared through toward a second entrance a bit further along. Through the hedges I could see that she had stopped by a bench and was stretching out in preparation for her run. No wonder this woman looked fit and trim for her age.

I entered the park and walked along non-chalantly as she began running. When she had disappeared toward the river and into the trees I eased my way out of the park and returned to my car. Each night after that I sat at the corner pub, like dozens of others, hoping to catch another glimpse of the woman. I learned that every Monday, Wednesday, and Friday night she ran in the park. Same time. Same path. I felt I was ready to put my plan into action.

The next day I went to the sport shop and bought some running clothes. My idea was to go into the park looking like I was a runner so that even if I was seen with her it would appear that I belonged with her. It was a slim chance as Wednesday nights, the night I had chosen, the park was desolate. But, like I said I don't like to take chances.

I had checked out the park and chosen the spot for our "encounter". It was near the centre of the park, far away from the roads and far away from houses. It was near a long line of trees that during the day formed a decorative archway, but by night became a long, dark corridor that only foxes dared retreat into. She had to run past the gaping maw of this tunnel twice during her run. I would get her on her second pass, when she was a bit winded, and less likely to be able to scream loudly.

Wednesday night I parked my car at one of the entrances near my chosen spot and walked around the perimeter of the park before entering it. Wearing my bright running sweats I looked just like anybody else going into the park for a run. I had arrived nearly half an hour before I expected her. I stretched out just like I had seen her do and then jogged a few yards before settling into a walk. I kept a sharp eye out for anyone else in the park. Near the entrance a man was walking his yappy little poodle, but they wouldn't be there very long. He probably lived in the neighbourhood and just took the mutt out before retiring for the evening. It was a perfect night. No moon and heavy clouds. There was a bit of a chill in the air, but not too much. When I reached my hiding spot I had one more quick glance and ducked into the deep shadows to wait. I didn't have to wait long.

I looked toward the bridge at the park's entrance and saw a long shadow, cast by the lights which lined the paved pathway. I could see her! She was moving in a graceful, easy stride. My pulse quickened as each step brought her closer to me. Soon I could see her more clearly. Her eyes were focused ahead of her, intent on the path, and her course. Suddenly I heard a loud noise beside me and something running through the brush! I was already so tense with desire that I nearly yelled out loud in shock. The woman must have heard it too and looked directly toward me. I froze. A fox burst out of the trees and into the meadow. Lucky for me the woman saw it too and was just as relieved as me. As she drew closer I could hear her rhythmic footsteps falling against the pavement and I could see her breasts bob in time to her gait beneath the shimmering fabric of her running suit. I didn't think I could bear to become any more aroused by my prospects. I crouched down in silence as she passed by my hiding place.

When my woman had passed I swiftly circled around out of the trees and made my way to the foot path. My plan was simple—I would start running toward her as though I too was simply in the park for some exercise. I heard footsteps approaching and looked up to see my woman approaching the trap I had set. I had timed it perfectly. We would reach one another at the very opening of my darkened lair. She raised her gaze to meet my eyes as we came closer. When we were nearly upon one another she began to smile but her eyes filled with alarm when I shifted my course to intercept hers. She had no time to react before my cupped hand closed tightly over her mouth and my large arms wrapped tightly around her body, clasping her arms to her sides. I nearly lifted her off her feet as I swept her into the surrounding darkness of the trees. I hurried her along the rough trail, half lifting and half dragging her body with me. We were many yards deep before she had time to try fighting me, but she quickly resigned herself to my powerful grip and my urges to keep moving.

When we were well-hidden from view I slowed down and put my mouth to her ear. I could smell her sweat and her perfume mingled together. Her body felt deliciously soft and yet firm as I pressed her helplessly to my side.

"If you try to scream I'll hurt you," I threatened. I gripped her more tightly. "Do you understand me bitch?"

This time she nodded slightly and I heard a muffled whimper under my hand. I already knew where I was going, but I needed a bit of light to find my way so gripping her head and mouth even more tightly I released her body and reached into my pocket for the tiny torch I had brought with me. She made no extra efforts to escape. She had become the mouse trapped by the cruel cat as it trembles in sharp jaws.

Twisting the torch on I saw the very tree I had picked earlier. It was large with a trunk about two feet in diameter leaning slightly to one side, covered in rough bark, and with two large limbs about five feet off the ground. I roughly shoved her against the tree, placed my large hand around her throat, and warned her again.

"If you scream or try to get free I'll hurt you like this."

I took my hand away from her mouth and wrapped both hands tightly around her throat. I could hear her gasping for breath as I gradually squeezed tighter and tighter. I could feel the flesh of her neck collapsing before slightly slacking my grip.

"Do you understand me?"

She nodded and I continued to hold her throat in one hand while my other fished around in my pocket for a length of strong rope. Her eyes flared when she saw the white rope flash by her eyes. I gripped her wrist strongly and tied the rope tightly to her wrist. While pressing her harshly to the tree I lifted her arm around the tree, above the first limb, and tossed the rope over. This was the riskiest moment, when I had to release her in order to step around the tree.

"Hug the tree—put your other arm over," I ordered with as much menace as I could muster.

She complied and I stepped around in a matter of a second or two. I pulled her bound arm tight with the rope and secured the loose end to her other wrist, pulling it taut and forcing her to arch her body and stand slightly on her tip toes. Stepping around I could see her tightly hugging the tree, her breasts flattened against the trunk. I had bound her to the tree so that she was forced to lean backwards. She whimpered as I stepped up behind her, pressing my body close to hers, and forcing the hardness of my cock against her arse. I couldn't wait to feel her helpless body beneath my hands. I wrapped one hand back around her throat and began to ruthlessly explore her body with the other. Her breasts were as lovely as I had imagined, full and heavy but with a youthful firmness and large erect nipples. I was not prepared for the firmness of her tummy and bum, a testament to her fitness I suppose. Maybe I imagined it but it seemed that she was responding to my touches by stroking back against my hand. Perhaps it was a trick—I don't know—but it spurred me on to satisfy my wants.

Releasing her throat I gripped her trousers in both hands and roughly jerked them down to her ankles, exposing her glorious pale skin to the chill air. She whimpered slightly.

"Silence bitch," was all I needed to say to keep her quiet.

I thrust my hand between her legs, forcing her to part them, and stroking the soft flesh of her cunt. She was shaven! I could feel the swollen lips of her cunt and the hard little pearl of her clit even with my rough hands. Even as I stroked I could feel her body respond. Her lips grew slick and full and a slight moan echoed from deep within. God how I wanted this woman. I wanted to fuck her ferociously!

I gripped the waist of her jacket and ripped it up over her breasts. Then I slipped my fingers under her tightly fitting sports bra and jerked it up beneath her arms, releasing her heavy breasts and hardening nipples. I pressed her back up against the tree, knowing that the rough bark would bite into her tender flesh. I took one of her large nipples into my fingers and began to roll it and pinch it while my other hand returned to her wet and swollen cunt. This time I couldn't resist forcing my fingers deeply inside her. She arched her arse out to meet my thrust and began to shudder with uncontrollable orgasms. *Victory*, I thought to myself as her body released itself to my control. I knew that I no longer needed ropes or threats of force to fuck this woman. I slipped more fingers into her, stretching her cunt tightly, and thrusting into her. She surrendered. She was all mine.

After a few minutes I stopped and watched her sag against the tree, her body trembling, her breathing ragged. Reaching up I quickly loosened one of her hands and pulled her away from the tree. I turned her around and slammed her back into the tree while bringing her wrists up and binding them tightly together with the rope. When the final knot was secure I forced her down onto her knees, facing me, and backed up to the tree's trunk. I pushed my own trousers down to my ankles and thrust my hard cock into her mouth. She tried to take only the tip, turning away in complaint.

"Suck my cock you slut. Suck my cock like your life depends on it. Taste my sweat."

Immediately my cock buried to the hilt in her mouth and I could feel the warmth of her flesh flow around my cock. I began to thrust in and out of her mouth and with each thrust heard a muffled cry from her. Her cries turned to deep moans as I felt my cock swell and the cum boil in my balls. I had half a mind to change my plans and fill her mouth and throat with my cum, but quickly decided that I wanted to possess her completely. There was only one way to do that. I pulled away from her with a pop and heard a moan of complaint escape her lips.

Gripping her hair I forced her onto her hands and knees into the wet, dark earth and leaves of the forest floor. Her arse was raised high in the air, her head bowed low, her breasts hanging lusciously almost to the earth. I stroked my hand over her cunt and felt that she was wet and open, just the way I needed her. Standing behind her I lowered myself and wasted no time before thrusting my cock deeply into her cunt. I could feel her flesh devour me as she drew me in deeply. I began to slowly thrust in and out of her, picking up the pace as my excitement climbed. Her jacket and bra was still up high beneath her arms, exposing her pale, ivory skin against the black earth of the night. I gripped her hips tightly and pulled myself deeply within her.

Suddenly I stopped. Only a few seconds passed before she began to thrust against me and grind in rhythm to my cock. I could feel her tightening as I began to thrust again. I could hear her suppressing groans of pleasure as my cock filled her. I could wait no longer and began to thrust savagely into her body. She thrust back just fiercely as the cum welled in my balls. Digging my nails into the tender flesh of her hips I held her tightly as my cum filled her cunt. Her body sagged wearily to the forest floor as I quickly pulled out of her and stepped away, my cum still dripping from my cock onto her back. I pulled my trousers up and turned to walk away. When I left her she was breathing heavily, her face buried in the earth.

L.M.H.

A Girl's Gotta Do
What a Girl's Gotta Do

It seemed I'd been job-hunting forever. Id gone on two interviews this morning—without luck of course—and had just now finished combing through the "Help Wanted" section of the newspaper. Once again I failed to find anything suitable. Frustrated and more than a little disappointed, I folded the paper back up and leaned back in my chair.

What am I going to do? I thought.

Rent was due in less than a week and I was flat broke. Id been laid off more than a month ago and had been hopelessly looking for work ever since.

Sighing quietly, I reached over for my cup of coffee. From the corner of my eye I noticed a small ad near the bottom of the page that I hadn't seen before. The words *FIRST PRIZE—$10000* caught my eye right away, so I picked up the paper to see what it was about.

Amateur Dance Contest
Tonight
Harley Rules Bar
FIRST PRIZE $1000

At first I dismissed the ad. *Who would do that?* I thought plainly. But then I realized that I didn't exactly have a whole lot of options. I was going to have to do that if I wanted a place to live. With that thought in mind, I picked up the newspaper one more time and took a long look at the ad. Breathing deeply, I resolved to do it. A girl's gotta do what a girl's gotta do these days, I thought. Besides, what do I have to lose? The place is clear on the other side of town. No one will even know me

The evening came quickly and, not knowing quite what to expect, I'd worn just a plain white cotton sundress with nothing underneath. My milky white legs were cleanly shaven and I'd chosen a pair of white platform sandals to complete the outfit. I was feeling pretty confident, but after seeing all these other women, my stomach was turning nervously, especially now as I watched a pretty blonde fucking a beer bottle on stage.

How could she do that in front of all these people?, I thought and, more importantly, how am *I* going to do that?

I looked to my right to ask my friend Lori, whom I had brought for moral support, when I heard the girl on stage scream out in obvious ecstasy.

The bouncer, having also heard the blonde, looked sternly at me and said, "You're up kid."

I glanced at Lori nervously. Always a friend, she smiled reassuringly and said, "You'll be a hit. Don't worry!" Then she disappeared into the audience.

After taking one last drink of my margarita, I walked on stage. The music I'd requested began to play so, figuring I had nothing to lose, I began to dance.

I closed my eyes and let myself get lost in the music. My hips were moving to the sensual Latin beat and my hands were smoothing up and down my arched torso, beginning just beneath my taut breasts, down over my stomach, to just above my mound. It was so hot up here with the lights and the sweat that I decided it was time for me to shed my dress. Slowly turning around, my hips never faltering in their dance, I proceeded to pull my dress up inch by inch, until it seemed that even I could hardly stand the anticipation anymore. Breathing hard, I lifted the dress up over my head and let it drop to the floor.

Oops, now I have to pick it up! I thought excitedly. I couldn't believe how hot this was making me! I don't think I'd ever been so turned on in my life!

I spread my legs just a bit and bent over at the waist, making sure to keep my legs straight, and happily exposed my tight asshole and dripping pussy to the cheering crowd.

From this angle, I was able to see the upside down crowd from between my legs and I happened to notice Lori sitting near the back of the bar. Her jet-black hair shined silver beneath the lights and her dark skin glowed as she watched me dance. Our eyes met and I knew she wanted me. I also knew that I wanted her, too. We'd often talked about experimenting with other girls, but neither of us had ever had the balls to do it—no pun intended!

Unthinking and uncaring now, I stood up and turned around, eliciting cheers and whistles from the men. My song had not yet ended, so my naked body continued to flow with the beat. I got even more into it, though, as my eyes again met Lori's. I began dancing for her. I grabbed at my breasts and kneaded them, pinching my pierced nipples. Then I let my left hand stray down until it dipped into my hot pussy. I was so wet! I rubbed it for a little bit, then brought my finger up to my mouth and licked it clean. Lori visibly jumped at this and I knew I had to have her.

Jumping off of the stage, the bouncer protecting me, I made my way to where the raven-haired beauty was sitting. Still somewhat unsure, we just stared at one another for a few moments, but I could no longer take the arousal. My hands, seemingly of their own accord, moved up to caress her face. She leaned forward and we kissed for the first time. Her lips were so soft and sweet, so unlike a man's. I wished this could go on forever, but I wanted to taste her. I broke our kiss and moved my lips downward to nibble on her neck as my hands busily unbuttoned her blouse.

Meanwhile, the music had stopped, but I don't think anyone in the club noticed, much less minded. The men encircled us, no longer cheering, just all breathing heavily. They wanted this as much as Lori and I did.

As soon as I'd finished with her buttons, I opened her blouse to reveal those lovely breasts that I'd admired so many times before. I wanted so desperately to slowly tease those beautiful nipples, but I just couldn't help myself. I bent over and took one in my mouth right away. I suckled it like a baby until I felt it grow hard under my tongue and then moved to the other one. She moaned softly and I did the same, unable to keep my pleasure in. All the while, my hands were caressing the smooth skin of her stomach and playing with her belly button. I continued to do this until I felt Lori's hand on my head, pushing me down. Eagerly I took her hint and spread her legs wide. She was wearing a short, black mini-skirt and, as I discovered, no panties.

Her pussy was shaved and soft. It glistened beneath the lights and it seemed to twitch as I flicked it for the first time with my tongue. I couldn't believe how awesome this felt, to be able to bring my best friend such pleasure. She was squirming beneath me as I licked her silky, pink folds. It tasted so sweet, better than I'd ever imagined. Slowly, I inserted a finger into her vagina and felt it instantly contract around my finger. I pushed into her over and over, loving the squishing sounds her pussy made each time. She was screaming wildly, bucking on my hand and tongue, and I knew she was close. I began to work her clit faster and faster with my tongue when suddenly I felt a cock being shoved hard into my pussy. Immediately taking my face from Lori's cunt, I looked behind me to see the bouncer fucking the shit out of my pussy.

It felt so good and I was about to give into the pleasure, but then I remembered my task. I looked back to the gorgeous pussy in front of me and again began lapping at it. It didn't take any effort at all this time though, as Lori came almost instantly all over my face. I continued licking her until she pulled my face from her pussy and kissed me.

As our lips parted, she whispered, "Look around!"

I did, and saw that almost every guy there had his cock in hand, stroking as they watched the show. God, it turned me on so much to know that all these guys were turned on watching us.

Meanwhile, I was still relishing the feel of the bouncer's cock pounding relentlessly into me and was eagerly thrusting my hips back to meet him when he came, screaming, inside of me. I could feel his hot seed running down my thighs as he pulled out and I instinctively scooped up a bit with my finger and brought it to my mouth. Lori, seeing this, and apparently not wanting to be left out, got up out of her chair and began eating his cum out of my pussy like there was no tomorrow. When there was none left, she laid me down and began to finger me while moving her tongue quickly over and over my ripe little bud in tiny circles. My hips moved eagerly to meet the thrusts of her tongue and fingers. I couldn't take much more. All I could think about was my best friend's magnificent tongue in my pussy.

"Oh God this feels so good—mmmoh yes oh yes oh yesaaahhmmmmmSHIT." I was screaming incoherently now as I shifted wildly beneath her.

Then, suddenly, with a shrill scream, my climax took hold and my body tensed. She knew I was coming, but didn't stop. She continued to vigorously eat my pussy, giving me an endless stream of mind-shattering orgasms. I was in so much pleasure that it nearly hurt. I just lay there, kneading my tits and rolling my head from side to side. I was exhausted and shivering uncontrollably, feeling those little aftershocks of pleasure course through me, letting them occupy my reality for awhile. But then, eventually, they subsided and my eyes opened. She kissed me yet again. My pussy tasted so sweet on her lips.

It was at that moment that I felt the first spurts of cum hit my body. At first I was confused, but then I remembered where we were and what we were doing. I looked around and saw that the men had decided to shoot their loads on Lori and me. Still aroused, we took turns licking it off of each other's bodies

Later that night, as Lori and I walked out of the club $1,000 richer, she turned to me smiling and said, "To think you were shy at first! Ha! I knew you'd be a hit!"

Stephen Van Scoyoc
Sam and Me Make Three

"God, I hate this job!"

I never figured I'd end up this way. Hell, I was the prom queen—had guys creamin' in their shorts just to get close enough to smell my freshly washed hair. Now the only crown I'm wearing is this stupid hat at the Taco Queen. I used to wear a cheerleader's uniform two sizes too small so all the guys on the team would notice my firm breasts. I used to love listening to the geeks try to ask me out on a date before tellin' 'em "no way!" to their face. Now? Well, I'd rather not get into that. Let's just say at this point I'd be happy with a geek.

I spend my whole shift at the deep fryer, dunking in frozen tacos, draining 'em, and passing them over to pimply-faced Todd so he can put the regulation lettuce and secret sauce on 'em. It ain't no secret—I know what's in it—and believe me, you don't wanna know. I'd been doing this for over a year and was still only making minimum wage and workin' all the shitty shifts.

Now that prick of a manager, Greg, was making me come into work again—on my day off! I hadn't even had time to wash my clothes—they still stank like the floor at the Taco Queen—now they were stickin' to my skin from all the grease and my sweat. Definitely not sexy. Greg used to be okay when he was captain of the football team, but he blew his knee and next thing I knew he was my boss and he hated my guts.

He used to think I was okay too when he fucked me in the back of his Camaro—yeah—the same crappy car he still drives. I can't count the times I laid on that cramped back seat while his heavy, sweaty body pounded my poor snatch. Well, pounded is a bit optimistic. I've always been such a good girl and never told anyone that he lasted all of about five seconds in my tight, young cunt. I used to go home, lock myself in the bathroom, and frig my clit until I finally popped myself off.

Now that Camaro ain't so bitchin' with all that dull blue paint peelin' off and the upholstery in shreds. Instead of roaring and smoking tires when the lights change it just knocks and belches black smoke while the shiny new Mazdas zip by. The girls don't line up by it anymore either, droolin' all over him, and wishin' he'd take 'em for a ride. Nah—he's as bad off as me.

After I got all dressed I drove my piece-of-shit Toyota through this piss-ant town yet one more time and stared at all those pathetic people I was gonna leave behind when I went to the big city, but it seems like only two of us stayed behind—me and Greg. It still looks like a *Leave it to Beaver* town and—can you believe it—they're *proud* of it! What the hell am I still doin' here?

I pulled into the parking lot at the Taco Queen, my tires squealing on the hot pavement. It's almost outside of town, next to the grain elevators that don't work anymore. Sort of like Greg's dick, just stickin' up in the air all useless and empty. Todd was out there changing the sign. He gave me that goofy gap-toothed smile and waved. What a twit. I smiled and waved back, pretendin' to be nice. Now the sign said "TrHee taCos 1 DolLer". What a fucking idiot. He's always gonna have a job with his name on his shirt. Oh well, only idiots eat at the Taco Queen anyway. They'll never notice.

"Christ it's hot," I thought to myself as I pulled my butt away from the hot plastic seat.

I could almost see the steam rising off the asphalt when I got out of the car. The ground was sticky from all the spilled drinks and greasy bags people had tossed on the ground. Yep—that's my job too. "Police the parking lot," Greg calls it. Crap picker-upper I call it. I walked into the joint. At least it was cool in there. It still stunk like old lard.

"You're late!" Greg hollered at me from behind the counter.

How about that! I smiled to myself. That prick was havin' to work the fryer himself!

"If you know what's good for you, you'll get back here and take care of this."

That's when I snapped. Oh it didn't happen all at once. More like one of those cartoons where the character starts filling up like a balloon, turns red, and then bursts all over the place into a jillion pieces. Real calm like I looked around at all the people munchin' on their tacos. They were lookin' at me too, wonderin' what I was gonna' do next. Seems I have a reputation. I looked behind the counter. Everyone had stopped. Even the customers in line had turned around to look at me. It all came over me kinda' slow like. I looked back at Greg with that stupid hat of his and the wonky badge that said "General Manager". He was standing there holding up a basket of greasy fries just looking at me like a dufus.

"Fuck you!" I screamed and shot my middle finger up to the ceiling. "Fuck you and your pathetic, limp little cock!" I added with a snort as the last bit of revenge. Then I turned around and stormed out the door toward my car.

As I went past his crappy blue Camaro I had a brilliant inspiration. I looked back at the Taco Queen. Nobody could see me except for Todd and he was still trying to spell "fEE coKe" on the big board. In no time at all I was squattin' on the driver's seat pissing for all I was worth. Thank God for generic beer. I'll never forget the sound of my piss hittin' the vinyl on his seat. It was like a thunderstorm on a tin roof. I could almost imagine it was boiling and steaming as it soaked into the tattered cushion. I was already fantasizing about what would happen when he sat in it.

I was just wringing out the last few squirts when I heard the door to the joint swing open with a bang.

"HEY—what the fuck are you doing!"

"Ooops," I said quietly to myself. Caught a bit earlier than I had planned. I snatched my thong back up my crack and leapt out of the car. I s'pose I could have run away, but something told me to stay and enjoy the moment. He was already lookin' inside the car and turnin' up his nose.

"You bitch—you're gonna pay for that!"

"Not on minimum wage I'm not!" was my witty reply. Well, I thought it was pretty clever at the time.

He grabbed me by the arms and began yelling right in my face. I didn't hear much of it, but I did catch the words "police" and "arrested." Hell, I didn't need no more trouble from deputy Bob so I figured I'd go along and agree to anything. I could leave town later if it got too hot and heavy. I guess I just didn't care anymore.

"What d'ya want," I finally asked as demurely as possible.

"I'll tell you what I want," he yelled. Then, softer, so no one else could hear. "I want a blow job from you—every Sunday." I nearly gagged just from the thought of taking that greasy smelling stale piece of meat into my mouth.

"Okay," I cooed. He probably thought this was turnin' me on.

"And pay for the seat!" he added.

I nodded in agreement.

He seemed pretty pleased with himself, but my mind was already goin' a hundred miles an hour 'cause I had me an idea.

"I have a better idea."

"Yeah? What's that?"

"How'd you like a threesome with me and my girlfriend?"

I knew I had 'im hooked before he even opened his mouth.

"When? Who?"

"Sunday, at the *Rancho Drive-Inn*."

"Who with!" he repeated.

"Sam—Samantha—you don't know her but she's a plenty hot number."

"Yeah, well, okay. I'll get the room—you better be there!"

"Oh I wouldn't miss it for the world!"

I couldn't wait to get home and call Sam. I'd met her the year before and we still hung out from time-to-time. I rang her up and told her what I had in mind. She giggled and said it would be great fun. Now, mind you, there ain't nothin' 'tween me and Sam. We're just friends. We spent a few more minutes talkin' 'bout what we'd wear and said our goodbyes.

Sam met me at my house and we drove to the *Rancho Drive-Inn*. Greg's Camaro was already parked outside one of the bungalows. I noticed with some satisfaction that his seat was covered in black garbage bags. I stifled down my laughter and knocked on the door.

"Come in bitch," his voice boomed from behind the door.

Sam and I walked in. We looked bitchin' man. I was dressed to kill in something I knew would hold Greg's attention. I still had the same body I had in high school and had managed to pack it all into a tiny t-shirt and shorts that had been washed in hot water and tumbled dry about twenty too many times. Sam was dynamite, but, even if I say so myself, she didn't look quite as good as me. I mean, she was sorta skinny and plain with little tits and almost no hips at all, but she looked mighty fine in that clingy red dress.

That horny bastard Greg was already in bed wearing nothin' but boxer shorts. I walked right up to him and planted my lips on his. I snaked my tongue down his throat and let my hand brush over his cock. Yep, he hadn't been gettin' any and if I wasn't careful he was gonna blow his load before I was ready for 'im.

Sam was already sittin' on the bed next to him. She looked at me and winked before putting her hand inside the fly of Greg's shorts. Greg moaned as her fingers curled around his stiff cock and began stroking up and down. Greg laid down and Sam wasted no time pullin' his shorts down to his ankles. Greg sighed as I pressed my breast against his chest and laid another wet kiss on him. His eyes closed and he groaned again as Sam swallowed his cock into her mouth. I could see her out of the side of my eyes as she bobbed up and down slowly on Greg's shiny, wet cock.

"Darlin'," I whispered in his ear, "I'm gonna take a few snaps of this cuz I bet it'll be a once in a lifetime for you."

He would have agreed to anything at this point so I reached over for my purse and pulled out my little camera. I stepped back from the bed and took some photos of Greg, all splayed back with Sam slurping on his cock like a happy pup with a bone.

"Come back over here," Greg said to me.

"Ohhhh baby, I'm getting' so turned on just watchin' you," I said as I started to stroke my breasts and massage my cunt through the tight shorts like a porn star in heat.

"Oh God, I just wanna watch you fuck Sam first and them I'm all yours."

That was all Greg needed to hear and he reached down and pulled Sam up next to him. I snapped a few more pics for the album and tried to control my growing excitement. I mean I was really on the edge at this point. Greg was about to blow his wad before he could even get it into Sam.

Greg got up on his knees between Sam's legs, hiked her dress up, yanked her panties down, and was just about to bump nasty when it happened!

Out sprang the most gorgeous, thick cock you will ever see in your life. I always admired that about Sam! How could a tranny have such a nice hunk of meat? I think Greg screamed, but I'm not sure. I was too busy takin' pictures and laughin' my ass off! In all the ruckus Sam sprung up from the bed, grabbed the camera, bent over and grabbed Greg's clothes and flew out the door. Greg sorta had that "deer trapped in the headlights" kind of look. Know what I mean?

"You fuckin' bitch!"

He had a pretty limited vocabulary for a while until it all sunk in. I just sat down and watched him rant and rave for while.

"You know," I teased, "I think I'll take those down to the Foto-Mart and get 'em developed. Maybe some enlargements too," I grinned.

When I saw the terror in his eyes I knew he was thinking clearly again. Dear, dear Angela worked there—his little, still virginal steady. Wouldn't she be impressed as the film rolled out of the Fuji machine? I wonder what quality control would think of that? Just how do you adjust the color for a huge purple cock? Suddenly he looked real dejected and I almost felt sorry for him—almost.

"What do you want?"

"I want a raise—fucker."

"Okay. What else?"

"I want weekends off."

He started to protest, but I just stared at him real hard.

"Okay. Anything else?"

I thought a minute as I was walking out the door and then turned to him.

"Yeah, pay for your own fuckin' seat!"

I slammed the door behind me and never even worried about how he was going to get home without his clothes.

Sam and I took the pictures to the next town over to get developed. Sam's cock came out real nice in those color photos. We had to ask for two or three 8 by 10s. We couldn't help it if three of Greg's old football buddies owned the store—could we?

Susan Van Scoyoc

Anyone, Anytime, Anywhere

"**We can get anyone, anytime, anywhere**" read the banner over the agency door. Martine looked up and grimaced inwardly. *If I had any scruples at all...,* she thought to herself. But Martine knew that scruples were only for those who could pay the bills. With two small kids and no man in the house, or family to help all of the bills came to her. How else was she supposed to make the money she needed?

She felt her skin crawl as Ted stroked her shoulder and then slipped his fingers just a little further down towards the curve of her breast. Martine shifted in her chair so that he stopped and Ted, as usual pretended, or perhaps even believed, he hadn't done anything out of line.

"You know what we need Martine, and you know how to get it. You'll be paid in cash, nothing to declare to the tax man, no strings"

"I know and I'll do it but I don't have to like it. He's a good man. I'd vote for him right now. He wants to improve schooling and chase those dead beat dads who don't pay child support. He even supports women's rights which is rare 'round here. I could do with help like that."

"Don't give me that bleeding heart routine. I have a business to run. Get your attractive little ass over to that convention hotel and don't come back 'til you have something on him." As Martine rose and turned towards the door she felt the sickeningly familiar pat of his hand on her ass.

Men, Martine thought to herself as she drove towards the convention hotel.

A full day later Martine was still watching congressman Snell as he pressed the flesh with his adoring local public. All she needed from him was a clue. Something she could use to snare him. But as she watched she could see no cracks in his public image. He was kind to children and animals and unlike Ted, he never put his hands uninvited on a woman's body. She had even approached him after dinner as instructed and tried all the usual tricks. You know the ones: seductive voice, low bustline, high hemline. Nothing worked. Snell seemed indifferent to her charms, unlike the usual men she was sent to seduce.

For the second night Martine headed alone to her room. She knew this was it—Ted might be so furious he wouldn't use her again. God, I need the money, she was thinking as she headed toward the lift. Martine was so absorbed with her worries she didn't see the discarded napkin on the floor and before she knew what was happening she stumbled, falling hard onto the floor.

Martine lay there for a moment, stunned the way adults are when they fall. She flinched. Her knee stung badly. She rolled over so she was sitting and as she did so saw trousers standing before her. She looked at her knee, grazed and bleeding through the huge hole in her stocking, then upward at the owner of the voice asking: "are you okay young lady?"

To her surprise it was the congressman. He seemed genuinely concerned and reached out a hand to help her up. But, observant as ever, Martine noticed a bulge growing in the front of those well pressed trousers. In an instant Martine decided to play the injury further, play out the helpless damsel in distress.

"I wonder if you could help me to my room, it isn't far"

Martine couldn't believe her luck as Snell held out his arm and readily agreed. She felt bad as she knew from this point on he was hooked—and all for being a nice guy.

As they reached the room so carefully prepared by her colleagues Martine lent even more heavily on the congressman's arm. "Would you open the door for me and just help me over to the bed so I can sit down?" Martine asked in her most helpless voice. And truth was her knee did hurt like hell. "Of course dear," Snell replied and held Martine closer as he carried more of her weight.

They reached the bed together and Martine was relieved to take the weight off her knee as the congressman lowered her down. As she sat opposite him she could clearly see the bulge in his trousers bigger than before. Which is it, Martine asked herself: the helpless female, the torn stockings or the knee injury itself? How do I find out?

She watched Snell's face carefully as she ran her finger around the hole in the stocking. "Look at this hole, I can't believe one stumble tore such a hole." No real interest there she observed. Next came "My knee really hurts. I know you have helped so much already but I wonder if you would get me a wet towel to clean it up with." In an instant Snell was in the bathroom. Martine could hear the tap running as she looked to check on the tiny eye of the video camera peeping from the vase of flowers opposite the bed. She knew that the technical boys from Blue Star Investigations were good and that the bugs and video would work, with each backed up by another somewhere in the room. It would be terrible to do what she was doing and then find the only video had failed, as she had when working for some of the cheaper agencies.

Martine turned her attention back quickly to Snell who was coming toward her with a damp towel. "Thank you for helping so much, I feel so helpless."

That did it! She could see his eyes light up and his face flush. Martine knew where to go from here. "I just can't seem to manage anything. How could I have tripped and fallen so easily? As she said this Martine reached for the towel but at the same time deliberately brushed her arm along the clearly defined bulge firming before her eyes. Snell took a sharp intake of breath and his eyes met Martine's.

"Let me help you," Snell offered as he sat next to Martine on the bed. He tenderly took her knee in his hand and wiped it with the damp towel. Martine played along. "You're so kind and helpful, is there anything I can do for you?" Martine reached forward and began to stoke Snell's chest beneath his now crumpled shirt. Snell closed his eyes for a moment and then, with a seeming crumpling of will, said "yes."

Martine wriggled closer and started to slip her fingers beneath the shirt, between the gaps of buttons. She was pleased with herself thinking this would be easy. "Good man commits adultery" headline and she would be home by midnight. Already Snell's breathing quickened in speed. Martine continued. "Do you often help such helpless women?" she murmured. Snell groaned and lowered himself out until he was laying fully stretched out on the bed. He seemed to be struggling with something, but Martine was unsure of the source of the struggle. Perhaps he really is the nice guy they all talk about she thought to herself. She ran her hand over his trim body and down towards his belt buckle. She undid Snell's belt as he lay there and then slipped her hand down to his firm cock.

The moment she touched his cock he turned. She caught a glimpse of his eyes just as they changed so she had a moment to brace herself before the first blow fell. When she watched the video later Martine still wondered at how fast everything changed. She had been leaning over him and the next moment he was on all fours straddling over her body. He slapped her across the face. "You whore—all women are whores," as he ripped at her clothing. "Pretending to be helpless when all the time they want to be fucked."

Martine lay there dazed, both from the blow which left her cheek, nose and eye screaming in pain, but also from her complete loss of control. She realised that whatever Snell wanted to do now, she was powerless to stop it. Even with the video and bugs in the room she knew she was alone. After all, no one had thought this man would be anything other than a simple fuck. They had all prepared for a straight or even kinky fuck but not prepared for anything else. Martine could do nothing. She lay there powerless and helpless. Only a long time later did

Martine realise that this man's sexual drive hinged on a woman's power-lessness and helplessness.

To her horror she saw the belt she herself had unbuckled raised above her ready to reign blows down upon her. She raised her hands over her face whilst her breasts, stomach and exposed legs received the stinging blows of the leather strap. Martine instinctively tried to curl up into a ball, but could not as Snell had placed his weight over her knees, unbalancing and immobilising her. She lay there, protecting herself as best she could and thanking god that the buckle was in his hand and not biting into her flesh. As he rained down blows he was muttering between clenched teeth: "You whore. You're just like all the others. Those bloody single mothers who plead poverty but are fucking every-thing in trousers for money. All those begging letters asking for my sup-port. My wife, who can do nothing for herself. Nothing. It's always what I can do for her. And she never seems available for a good fuck. Never. Well, I know how to get one. All those star struck teens, those helpless women just need the feel of leather and a few good bruises to remind them…"

Martine shut her mind from what was happening as Snell muttered on and on about women and his wife. Through the beating she started to find a separate part of herself which was untouched. She had come here to fuck this man and to do this she often switched to a place inside herself. But this time she had something else.

This will end soon and then…then I will have a tape. I'm going to make this bastard pay for this, Martine thought. Not once did she think her life was in danger although hours later she wondered why she had not feared that too. Perhaps it was because as soon as he had finished hitting her he made it clear what he wanted. He wanted the fuck she had expected to give him. He wanted it, the fuck he claimed all women wanted and positioned himself to thrust into Martine. Martine closed her eyes knowing what to expect when she heard a guttural grunt and felt the wet warmth of his cum splashing onto her upper thighs. The congressman slumped over her, his weight continuing to pin her to the bed.

An eternity went by but it was probably only a few minutes before he raised himself and redressed himself. He looked over at Martine and asked: "So, you got what you wanted?"

Martine did not answer. The congressman seemed to think everything was normal. That all that had happened was not only acceptable but normal. The welts from the belt were burning a vivid red over her body and her check still stung from that one sharp blow. The congressman reached into his jacket pocket, took out a bundle of notes and threw them over Martine's motionless body.

"Here, that should cover it darling. If you want some more I will be at this hotel again next week." He turned and left.

Martine lay still, unable to believe what had happened and even worse, how Snell believed this was all normal between men and women. She reached out to the telephone by the bed and called the agency. She had done her job.

Next she dragged herself into the bathroom and ran herself a deep warm bath. She thought about Ted at the agency. At least he was open about what he wanted. As she lay there and saw the welts and beginning of the bruises she knew what she was going to do. It wouldn't just be Snell's opponent who would be using this information.......

Stephen Van Scoyoc
A Night in Benidorm

It has been a wonderful week and last night was our last night—today we fly back to London. We had been blessed with wonderful weather even though it was February in the Mediterranean seaside town of Benidorm, Espana. We always choose to take our holiday here in the winter when kids are in school and parents are at work. The beaches are deserted and, although it's too cold to swim or sunbathe, it is warm enough and sunny enough to chase away the gloomy memories of winter in England. Besides, it's much, much cheaper in the winter—a mere £99 per person including airfare and a luxurious flat overlooking the blue-green sea.

We thought we had seen everything the town had to offer, but one thing we had not yet found was a leather jacket for Sian. Spain is famous for its leather jackets, but the only ones we had found were cheap and tatty, made especially for the tourists, and cut to fit the broad backsides of the Germans. Sian was too petite, too trim, and too lovely to be seen in one of these pale imitations. Still, we carried on in the hope that we might chance across something.

On our last day exploring the older part of the city we entered a narrow, cobbled street with white stucco-walled buildings, colourful awnings, and small shops. It was like stepping back several hundred years in time. Sian's eyes lit up as she spied a leather shop with rack upon rack of leather jackets. It was getting late and many of the shopkeepers were already clearing their street displays and shuttering their doors. The aroma of tanned leather nearly made us swoon as we stepped into the cosy shop and began looking at the selection. The leathers were gorgeous—buttery soft and warm to the touch.

A young Spanish woman was quick to spy our interest and came straight over. She spoke nearly perfect English seasoned with her native Catalan. We were looking at women's jackets so she immediately turned her attention to Sian, stepping back to eye her size, and even running her hands over Sian's shoulders and waist with a practised expertise. As the woman bent over toward Sian I caught a playful wink from Sian who, I knew, got as much of a thrill from this woman's touches as any red-blooded young man would. This woman was just Sian's type. Petite, young, dark of skin, eye, and hair and with a body to die for.

The woman quickly selected three jackets for Sian, but put one back after stealing one more quick glance at Sian.

"What do you think of these?" she asked as she handed one of them to Sian.

Sian put it on, but it didn't seem to "hang" quite right over her ample breasts and tiny waist. The woman tutted and helped Sian out of it. She handed the other one to Sian.

Sian wriggled gleefully into the jacket with a giggle. It was made of the softest lamb leather and dyed a deep black. It had numerous pockets with silver zippers and a waist belt and buckle to cinch it tight around her waist. Sian zipped it up and the leather moulded snugly to her delicious body. The woman smiled with satisfaction and stepped behind Sian to examine the fit. Sian and I were both surprised when the woman began to brush her hands sensually over Sian's body, smoothing the leather over her shoulders, her back, her waist, and finally, over the swell of her breasts.

"It's perfect for you!" the woman beamed as she stepped back and admired Sian's figure outlined beneath the supple leather. The look on Sian's face told me it was sold!

We followed the woman over to the counter while an older clerk took our credit card and prepared the transaction. As we waited, the young woman began asking about our holiday, where we were from, etc. We told her, half jokingly, that we had thought Benidorm had a hopping night scene, but we hadn't found it yet. She took on a serious expression, looked at Sian, looked at me, and looked at the other clerks before stepping closer to us and taking our arms.

"Would you like me to show you around tonight?" she asked earnestly.

Sian and I looked at each other, looked at her, and nodded vigorously.

"Meet me outside in twenty minutes. We'll get something to eat and then I'll show you a good time. A time to remember."

We finished our transaction and she followed us to the door, reminded us to be there in twenty minutes, and locked the door. The lights went off in the shop almost immediately.

True to her word, the young woman appeared from a side alley about twenty minutes later. She too was wearing a skin tight leather jacket, buttoned up over her young curves, and in a lovely burgundy colour. Her short, curly black hair bounced around the jacket's collar and her dark eyes flashed in the coloured street lights.

"My name's Tiana," she said as she joined us. Introductions were made all around and Tiana started walking up the street toward a section where all the lights were still bright and music could be heard drifting along the stone walls. Tiana ushered us into one of the many small restaurants that lined the nearly empty streets. It was obviously a favourite of hers. We let Tiana do the ordering because even though we knew a bit of Spanish we had quickly learned that Spanish was seldom spoken here—Catalan was spoken instead.

We learned that Tiana had just finished her degree at university and was helping her parents out in their shop until she planned her next move. We quickly moved on to what she had planned for us. There was a mischievous gleam in her eyes as she told us about the night clubs that opened about 10.00 PM and put on risqué shows. We had heard of these—read about them in the travel guide. The real fun, Tiana said, didn't start until midnight when they locked the doors and nobody could come in or go out until about 5.00 AM in the morning. I wasn't sure I was up to it, but at the same time was deadly curious about what Tiana was up to. We readily agreed and she seemed very pleased.

About this time our meal arrived in a huge, steaming pan. Although we didn't recognise the language we recognised the dish—paella—one of our favourites! It was made with a lot of pride and full of seasoned rice, vegetables, and a bountiful variety of seafood. Sian and I didn't conceal our delight and thanked Tiana for her choice. We talked enthusiastically throughout the meal about her life in Spain and our lives back in England. She was delightfully witty and fun to be with.

We had finished our second pitcher of Sangria and I know I was beginning to feel the effects of both that and the arousing company of my two women companions. We paid for our meal and Tiana told us it was time to head for the club. She said she knew of a really fun one hidden among the many small side streets—one the tourists never found and wouldn't be let in to anyway. I should have been suspicious at this point but, as a stranger in a strange land, I was trusting of my host. Besides, Sian seemed to be having the time of her life. If I hadn't had so much to drink I might have remembered that Sian and Tiana had been laughing riotously upon my return from the toilet. They had quickly hushed up when I returned, but I had thought nothing of it at the time.

We came to an ancient wooden door set into the thick walls. I could hear music and the rumble of a crowd behind the heavy planks. Tiana banged heavily on the door with her shoe several times before the door creaked open a few inches. The loud sounds within boomed out onto the street and the odour of smoke and alcohol wafted out beyond the portal. Tiana said something to the gorilla of a man and he opened the door wide. I tried to follow Tiana and Sian, but the man barred my way and said something rude in Catalan. I was confused. Tiana turned to the man and began speaking quickly to him. His face wrinkled up and then smoothed out into a smile as he cast his eyes my way and dramatically ushered me in with a flourish of his hand.

"What did you say to him?" I asked Tiana. Sian just giggled and Tiana pretended not to hear me over the din. I followed along in growing bewilderment.

As we entered the main room I noticed that it consisted of a glass dance floor with flickering lights beneath and dozens of tables surrounding it where people were seated and drinking. There were quite a few women dancing to the latest mixes. That's when it hit me full on. They were all women. Not a man in sight unless I looked at my own reflection in a mirror. I stopped and noticed that Tiana and Sian were both looking at me with huge grins.

"All right—what's going on," I insisted.

Sian was the first to speak.

"It's an all-male revue," she said nonchalantly, waiting for it to sink in.

Tiana leaned in closer to me, pressing her breast against my arm.

"You're one of the dancers!"

I was stunned. What could I say?

I noticed a growing number of the women were casting inquisitive glances my way. Then I heard a male voice behind me, one I didn't understand. Tiana looked at me and motioned for me to go with him. I resisted. Sian stepped close to me and pressed her body sensually against mine. I could feel her breath upon my ear.

"We'll make it worth your while," she teased.

Tiana pressed up against me on the other side and whispered pleadingly in my ear.

"Please?"

Maybe it was the alcohol coursing in my veins or the prospects that awaited me if I went through with it, but I finally agreed and followed the bouncer like a bull into the arena. He led me to a small room packed with young men oiling their bodies and carefully putting on "rip-off" clothing like those I had seen in *The Full Monty*. I felt terribly out of place and appreciated how those middle-aged characters in the movie must have felt stripping for hordes of screaming women.

The men all turned to look at me—obviously wondering who the hell I was. The bouncer pointed to a box with a variety of "rip-off" articles. He said something to the men and they all turned away to finish dressing. They weren't interested in me. The gorilla grunted, turned, and strode out of the room. I stood in dismayed silence for a few minutes, trying to stop my head from spinning.

The men were all solidly muscled and evenly tanned. Not a one was over twenty-five. It reminded me of my childhood days when I had optimistically pasted a photo of Charles Atlas on my wall and lifted weights in hopes of developing those powerful looking arms, that solid chest, and a washboard stomach. It was all in vain. I got stronger than an ox—was probably stronger than any of these guys—but all I got was thick—like an ox. Instead of looking like Charles Atlas I ended up looking like a Russian weight lifter—like a barrel with legs and arms. Still, I had carried on because it had other benefits like making it possible to hold my lover in any position as we fucked each other senseless. The gorgeous bodies of these men were the least of my worries though. They were all clearly hung like stallions—swinging dicks like tree trunks—bigger than anything I had ever seen in a Soho sex shop. I wondered if there were really any women who could take such a monstrous cock. Maybe their cocks shrank with an erection? The thought brought a smile to my face as I looked down to compare myself. My smile evaporated.

These women had obviously come to see male pride at its finest as well as huge cocks barely hidden behind tight little elastic pouches. Now, my own cock is about average when erect and Sian had always seemed quite satisfied, even complimentary, but the rest of the time there isn't much to behold—or even hold. In fact, at that moment, my cock cowered like a kitten in a thunderstorm and no amount of coaxing would tempt it out into the open.

I sorted through the box and realised there was nothing in it for me. I would look more ridiculous trying to imitate these studs than not. I needed a clever plan—an act to follow.

The room was emptying as the men filed one-by-one into an adjoining room next to the dance floor. I later discovered that there was a one-way mirror so the men could watch the floor as the action took place. They reminded me of girls waiting their turn for a beauty pageant. I snickered to myself. Then I had an idea!

I quickly stripped out of my trousers and took off my shorts which I dropped ceremoniously into the box of other clothes. I fitted my trousers back on and carefully zipped them most of the way up. Rummaging around on the dressing tables I found some white makeup and smeared it thickly on my face. One of the men had left some thin black leather motorcycle gloves on the table so I quickly slipped them on. It wasn't perfect, but I figured the women would get the idea that I was a "mime" like the one I had seen in Paris. I must have been quite a sight when I stepped into the waiting room. I weathered out the stares and waited until the men's attention had returned to the dance floor where the first group was performing to the obvious delight of nearly a hundred screaming women of all ages.

It was easy to get caught up in the excitement and my mind was working effortlessly now, putting together my act. I noticed that as the men finished their performances they would line up along one side of the dance floor like meat on display in a butcher's shop, wearing only those tiny little pouches. I could use that to my advantage, I thought with some satisfaction. I hoped that I would be the last performer, but I didn't need to worry because these guys didn't take me seriously for a minute. Who would? A little middle-aged man in street clothes and a face like a clown surrounded by all these virile hunks? What's to worry?

Soon I was the only one left in the room and I had my first case of the butterflies as the act on the floor wound up. Wow, the atmosphere was incredible. The women were going crazy and clapping for the next act—which was me.

I opened the door slowly and stepped out into the dazzling light. The music stopped. The clapping died away. The screaming became a dull murmur as I stood there. I froze. Then I began to move in the jerky way of a puppet on strings as I turned to face the DJ, cocked my head, put my cupped hand to my ear, and waited. The DJ was certainly on the cue and immediately started up the music again. I began to move again in that agonizingly slow, mechanized way. Instead of heading for the centre of the dance floor I kicked my shoes off and targeted the first young stud in the row as he stood at parade rest, wearing only his little pouch, with his hard-on at full staff. I'll do him credit, he stood rock solid as this hideous being approached him. I stopped beside him and looked him over, mimicking his chest with my hands, and finally bending down close to his huge erection. Finally, giggles began to break out in the crowd and shouts in a language I didn't understand. I then moved on to the next stud and measured his erection with my eyes. The women were starting to clap to the beat of the music. I pulled off a sock and draped it across his barely hidden cock and moved away.

I jerked along to the largest, most muscular man in the row and studied him before turning to the audience. Slowly I removed my shirt, flexed my muscles in a caricature of body builders I had seen perform. Then I turned to him and invited him to copy me which—in good spirit and with a grin—he did! The crowd became riotous with laughter.

Now I reached the part I was most worried about—coaxing my poor cock into giving a decent performance. My eyes sought out Sian. I missed her at first because she was locked in a deep kiss with Tiana and her hands were stroking over Tiana's breasts. I felt a surge in my pants. Ahhh—just what I needed. Sian pulled away and looked over at me with a wicked smile followed by Tiana who was licking her lips. There was a growing flicker of life beneath my denim jeans. I no longer noticed the women in the crowd, only the two scrumptious bodies of my companions as they stroked one another for my benefit.

I turned one last time to gaze in animation at the row of erections behind me and in one swift motion let my trousers drop to the floor. There was an audible gasp from the women followed by thundering applause as my modest cock, reared in its fullest glory, bared itself to the flashing spot lights. The men behind me must have thought I was quite a spectacle because they could only imagine how big I was! They must have thought the worst!

I saw Tiana standing and starting to drift seductively toward me in time with the music. Sian wasted no time in following. I noticed that Sian had unzipped her jacket and was wearing only a black bra—one of my favourites—beneath it. It was a delicious blend of black leather, lace, and ivory skin. My cock twitched in anticipation of their arrival. A bouncer started to move toward them, but I shook my head slightly and he stood back. Both women reached me and Tiana put her arms around my neck, pressed her mouth to my ear, and said slowly:

"Let's give them a *real* show!"

I felt fingers stroking my cock and, remembering to move like a mime, looked down to see Sian face-to-face with my cock. I nearly collapsed when I felt her mouth close around my flesh. Out of the side of my eye I noticed the men behind me becoming restless and uneasy—like sheep when the wolf is about. It flashed through my mind that they were probably all like champagne bottles ready to blow their corks! This excited me even more, but not as much as the sensation of Tiana slowly kneeling to join Sian in licking and sucking my hard—if modest—cock. I felt the full length of my cock disappear into somebody's mouth and knew right away it wasn't Sian's. I nearly gasped as my cock, which had been cool and dry in the open air, was now warm and wet in Tiana's mouth.

Sian reappeared at my side with a satisfied look on her face and glistening drops of pre-cum on her lips. She nuzzled my ears and spoke to me as Tiana maintained a rhythm to the music. With each beat I felt myself coming closer and closer to the rapture.

"I want you to cum in her mouth," she cooed before putting her lips to mine and snaking her tongue in deeply. The crowd roared in approval—or disbelief—I didn't know or care which. I was oblivious to everything except the overpowering rush of my orgasm approaching.

"I want to see your cum dripping from her mouth," Sian continued to tease before flicking her tongue in my ear. Her hands were all over me. Tiana was cradling my balls in her hand as her mouth stroked me in and out. She must have felt me quickening as she wrapped her fingers around the shaft of my cock and sucked furiously on the swollen head. I let out a roar as the cum rushed through my cock.

Tiana never missed a stroke, but unlike Sian, who swallows every drop of my cum, Tiana swallowed some and used the rest on her hand to lubricate my cock so she could continue to pump me. I didn't think I would ever stop cumming. My knees nearly buckled under the intense pleasure I was feeling.

I started to come around and looked down at Tiana. Her leather jacket was spotted with patches of my cum and large drops glistened on her cheek and chin. She smiled up at me and held the weight of my only slightly relaxed cock in her hand. I was aware of the crowd standing, jeering, and applauding. I never even thought to look behind me. Tiana stood and kissed me with my own cum on her lips and we turned, arm-in-arm to face the crowd. The music started to play and the women began crowding onto the dance floor to gyrate to the beat.

"Fuck me—NOW!" Sian yelled at me over the music as she grabbed my hand and started dragging me toward the toilets. Tiana followed eagerly into the small room which was, not surprisingly, empty. Sian kissed me furiously on the lips, fucking my mouth with her tongue, before breathlessly telling me once again to fuck her, fuck her hard.

Sian was wearing a clingy black skirt over suspenders, stockings, and panties which matched the bra beneath her jacket. Sian bent over the sink, raising her arse towards me. I roughly hiked her skirt up over her waist and literally ripped her panties down over her legs and off of her ankles. Sian arched her back and thrust her cunt toward me. Her silky, shaven lips were wet and ever so inviting. My cock drew along her wet lips once and then slipped deeply inside in one smooth stroke. Sian thrust back and began to grind against my cock. I could feel her fingers brush against the base of my cock as she stroked along the side of her clit. I knew she was going to cum hard.

Remembering Tiana I glanced over to see her back pressed against the wall, shoulders scrunched up, her eyes glazed, one hand buried deep in her trousers, and the other rolling her nipple between her fingertips. My cum was starting to dry on her jacket. Her mouth was parted slightly and every few seconds her eyes would clear, take a look at me fucking Sian, and glaze over again.

Between gasps of breath Sian was screaming "FILL—ME—NOW—!!!" One more look at Tiana shuddering and thrusting against her own hand sent me over the edge. I gripped Sian's hips tightly, pulled her deep, and flooded her cunt with what cum remained in my body. She screamed like death itself, gripping my cock within her cunt, and convulsing several times before finally resting on the cool porcelain sink. I was too exhausted to move and just stood there, feeling my cum trickle from Sian's cunt, as my cock finally began to soften.

I looked up in the mirror to see my body, wearing only a white, painted face and black leather gloves, standing over the tiny arse of my lover. Tiana was gently cooing and sighing against the wall. I saw a dozen faces peering in through the door at us and smiled. What else could I do? I pulled out of Sian and watched a flood of cum flow down her leg. One of the faces became a full body as a woman stepped through and handed me *most* of my clothes. I thanked her and quickly began pulling on my clothes.

As we prepared to walk out of the toilets I saw Sian's knickers on the floor, still wet with her cum, and stuffed them into my pocket. All eyes were focused on the dance floor as we walked out, unnoticed. The other strippers were dancing wildly with the women. Their night was just getting started. We headed for the door and the same brute of a man who had let us in discretely let us out again with a grin.

We walked along the silent streets laughing and talking about what had just happened. Sian looked at me, looked at Tiana, and I knew that our night was just starting as well. This trip had certainly turned out different from all our earlier ones. We would have to leave the kids behind more often!

Susan Van Scoyoc

Daredevil Construction

So here he is, Daredevil Construction himself. What does he think he looks like in those torn jeans, tussled hair and one gold earring?! I ask you—what do these men think when they walk out of their homes at the beginning of the day—do they think they are still on the football team? The years have taken their toll but this Daredevil obviously hasn't looked in a full length mirror recently.

"Stop it," I shouted inside my head. "Stop that man-hating rage. They aren't all going to run off with the local tart," and my thoughts wander to what it was like when Ray was still here. He would wander around the house in jeans and an old T-shirt and it was sexy. But now I know it wasn't enough for good ol' Ray because he split with the woman from the hair salon, the one with all the make up and high heels. So here I am left with this dilapidated old house and a heart full of empty dreams.

But I'm learning. I may have been slow but this time I want this he-man to work for less than he bargained for. My girlfriends—those without a man that is—tell me how the real world works. Flash some tit and these stupid men will drool. I guess it isn't that different from being married when you think about it… That's what they tell me now—but why didn't anyone warn me before? Those girlfriends have been so good to me and they promised to help me out with this one too. Lots of advice on what to do, how and when…

So I lean forward over the rail and flash off enough cleavage to drown in. Daredevil is as subtle as most of them and his eyes are fixed on my Wonderbra bust whilst talking about how much he will charge to repoint the house. Interesting how he can't look me in the eye when full breasts are just in front of his nose!

I look at him with that helpless, little girl look all us women have practiced for just such an occasion and say: "But I can't afford $15,000. My husband left and the house is just falling down. If I can't fix it up I won't have anywhere of my own."

I stepped forward just enough to disturb his fixed gaze. I can see the flush of his face and feel the heat of his body. I brush just the tip of my nipple against him as I walk past and into the house asking: "Tea?" He follows like a dog in heat. He smells like one too.

That smell of sweat and testosterone hangs in the air between us as I wiggle and grind my way round the kitchen. Daredevil is clearly interested as I umm and ahhh about the price. Accidentally I drip tea from my glass onto my chin, knowing what will happen next. A small stream of iced tea begins to make its refreshing way down my neck and into the valley between that Wonderbra cleavage. I can see his eyes riveted to the spot, the spot where the tea disappears from view. Trailing my finger along the cool wet line I put down my glass and move closer.

"I think I'll have to change, don't you?" as I reach down and smoothly pull my now sodden top off my body.

Well, what do you think happens next girls? I'm standing there in the skimpiest skirt—nothing more than a belt my mother would have said—and my reliable Wonderbra. Herzigova has nothing on me. Promise. You got it—Daredevil can contain himself no longer and reaches forward for a touch. I let him of course. Remember the dare now—how low a price can I get from this Daredevil.

So here we are, in the kitchen, locked in a steamy embrace. It's clear what Daredevil wants, but he isn't going to get it just yet. I have some haggling to do. I push him off just hard enough to stop him but give him the look that tells him all is up for grabs, at the right price.

"So how much you gonna charge for doing the house?"

"$15000," he replies. I reach out and stroke his groin firmly.

"How much?" I ask again.

He can hardly say anything by now, his eyes rolling and breathing coming in gasps.

"I gotta charge you lady," he says but then comes the turning point.

My girlfriends arrive on cue. Sheena wiggles in the doorway without knocking, takes one look and comes to stand just behind Daredevil.

"Still negotiating Sandra?" she asks and then reaches round to run her long fingers over Daredevil's chest. Kathy walks in moments later and comes over to give me a kiss—a deep throated kind which leaves Daredevil with a body and mind that's reeling. He thinks he's landed in seventh heaven as we all touch and press against each other and him.

I turn to him and ask for the last time: "How much?"

He looks at long-legged Sheena, dark dusky Kathy and voluptuous me and says "I'll take payment in kind—as long as I get a favour from each of you every day of work I put in." Us girls look at each other and nod in agreement. Without a word we close in on Daredevil. We haven't had a man in a long time now...

Stephen Van Scoyoc
"Kim"

It had all seemed so adventurous on the posters—"Join the Navy and See the World," it had promised. I had seen the world alright—and a bit more than I wanted to see. That's how I ended up in the hospital with the rest of my friends. It wasn't serious and I was only there a couple of days before they handed me my records and my orders to return to base in the US. It was all very hush-hush and I was given three months off without explanation.

I hobbled out of the hospital into a slightly chilly but sunny day in Spain. I had arrived in the dark by helicopter so really had no idea what part of Spain I was in. I was too disoriented to really care. I wandered over to the BEQ to check in, hoping to catch a few more winks of sleep. The past few weeks had really taken a toll. I arrived to find the open barracks in a flurry of activity as men, wearing only their white t-shirts and dungarees, busily scrubbed the floors and wiped down the bulkheads. It was a full-scale field day. I grimaced. I wouldn't be getting any rest here.

I handed my heavy packet to the petty officer on duty, a third class boatswain's mate. Without even looking at me he jabbed his finger out into the barracks and told me to "get busy with the other guys." I stood there until he noticed I was still there.

"What are standing there for? Get busy," he said with a menacing edge.

"Stand up," I said in a quiet voice.

When he didn't stand up, I repeated it more firmly adding a "now" to the end. Noticing now that I had a full arm of stripes, hash marks, and colorful ribbons pinned on my chest, he stood up a bit warily.

"I'm not gonna put you on report because I'm too fucking tired to mess around with you. I've been around too long to take orders from little pricks like you and I haven't swabbed a deck since I was seaman."

"Look, I'm sorry. We get guys in here all the time and the CO—he makes me put 'em to work. It's not my idea. If you're gonna stay here he'll expect you to do shit work."

"Fine—give me back my records."

"But, you won't have any place to stay and you won't have any meal chits."

He handed me my records without endorsing them. I had plenty of money and could eat at the base canteen. I had just spent nine months at sea and another month doing—well, doing something I still can't talk about. I'd make do. I headed on over to the airport to see if I could hop a quick flight back to the States.

I walked into the terminal and saw the rest of my team. I had been the last one out of the hospital. Some were curled up in chairs while others were sprawled out on the dirty floor sleeping. Kurt was at the counter trying to chat up one of the civilian clerks. I had to admit even after nine months at sea he wasn't too desperate. He had chosen the most attractive one, a youngish looking blond with short hair cut in a pixyish bob. I just laughed at the lanky, gawky guy and sat down next to "monk".

"What's happening?" I asked him.

"I dunno, we were 'sposed to leave yesterday, but there aren't any planes."

I was surprised at first, but when he mentioned it I realized I hadn't heard any large planes taking off—no C5's, C141s, not even C130's— just an occasional corporate style jet from time to time. I was the senior man present so I decided to ask around. I heard laughter and looked around to see that Kurt has "crashed and burned" with the clerk and was returning with a sheepish grin on his face while the guys guffawed and pointed fingers at him.

I dropped my seabag on the floor and walked up to the counter. The woman came over to me.

"Can I help you?" she asked in a pleasant voice, apparently not at all bothered by Kurt's shenanigans. She was probably used to it.

"Yeah, I've got orders to fly out of here—back to the States." I pushed my orders and travel documents across the counter. She took a quick look at them and pushed them back.

"I'm sorry, but there's been an emergency. There were some earthquakes in the Azores—all the planes and extra personnel are flying aid missions right now. I don't know how long it will be. It could be a couple of weeks. All you can do is keep checking in and we'll get you out when we can."

I was too tired to be annoyed. It must have shown in my face.

"You guys had a pretty rough time didn't you?"

I didn't know if she actually knew anything or was just guessing.

"Yeah, we're pretty bushed—just want to get home now."

"Have you guys checked into the barracks? You're going to need a place to stay—you can't stay here."

I looked back at her and smiled before speaking gently.

"Look, these guys have been sleeping on the floor in churches and in airplanes for weeks now. They don't really want to stay in a barracks and do shit work—not after what they've been through."

I looked at her as she glanced over to the men. They were a pretty motley crew.

"They won't bother anybody. Just let us stay here until we can fly out. If anybody gives you any grief just send to me—I'm in charge of them."

"Okay—say—you look like you've been hurt. Are you okay?"

"Yeah, I'm okay now—just really tired."

I stayed and chatted a while. Her name was Kim. She was twenty six—and she was American. She was attractive, but the most striking thing about her was her smile and her sparkling eyes. She didn't want to be here either. She and her husband had moved here to be missionaries a couple of years earlier. Her husband struck up a romance with some Navy seaman and followed her back to the states nearly eight months earlier, leaving Kim working a part time job and taking all their savings back with him. Kim was more stranded than I was. She earned just enough to pay the rent on her flat and buy food, but nothing left over to buy a plane ticket back to the States. I suddenly felt very tender toward her. She was being so nice to my men even when she had little left to hope for herself.

At about 2300 the terminal started to shut down and Kim prepared to leave. She worked rather odd shifts, she had said, usually the ones nobody else wanted. Most of my men were now sleeping, but I had been too wired up to rest. I walked up to say goodbye to Kim and asked when she would be back in. She was gracious and told me she would be back in at 1500 the following day. Frankly, I couldn't wait to see her again. She shot me another smile as she walked out the terminal and turned off most of the lights. The door closed behind her and I was left with the sound of wind whistling around the building and the snores of my men echoing off the walls. I laid down and tried to sleep, but was hurting all over in spite of the medication. The floor was cold and I had nothing but a coat to cover myself up with. Maybe I should have stayed and swabbed floors…

The activity in the terminal started early the next morning. A few of us left the terminal to eat at the chow hall. Nobody asked for chits so we just joined the rest of the base for breakfast. We returned quickly so that the others who had guarded our bags could go eat. We resumed our vigil in the terminal, hoping a plane, any plane, would come along and take us somewhere different. I was beginning to feel worse, my legs were swelling and throbbing, and my bandages had begun to show red where the blood had soaked through. I just popped some more pills, tried to ignore it, and nodded off in the hard plastic chair.

I came around in late-afternoon to see Kim smiling at me as she shuffled papers and manifests. There had been some planes in and out to refuel or take on cargo, but none with any room for passengers. I went up to talk to Kim. The situation hadn't changed. Maybe it was the medicine—I don't know—but I asked her if she wanted to leave Spain and return to the US. She said that she did but didn't know how. There was nobody she could turn to for money and no place for her stay in the US—nothing to get started with. I told her that in my line of work sometimes it was simpler to take chances and worry about the very next minute instead of the next hour.

"Can you get a ticket to New York?" I asked her. She looked stunned.

"If I skipped the rent and didn't buy groceries—yes, I could buy a ticket. Why?"

"You want to go back?"

"Yes, of course."

Her eyes were puzzled and she looked confused.

"Get yourself a ticket. Get to New York. I'll pick you up there."

I had a small house and several months off before I had to return to duty. I felt that would be enough to help her get on her feet again.

There was a long silence. I knew what was happening. Unlike the small team of men I was with, Kim had never had to trust someone she didn't know. The one person she had trusted had shafted her. I waited patiently.

"I don't know…" she wavered, a serious look on her face.

"You'll have to trust me," I said in deadly earnest.

Kim's eyes started to glisten with tears.

"I'll let you think about it. No conditions. Just be in New York. Let me know when. I'll be there."

Kim nodded her head and turned away. I limped back over to the guys. They had been watching me and then started kidding me, figuring

I was hitting her up. I just smiled and sat down with a groan. I started to doze again until about 1900. Brad was poking me, telling me to wake up.

"That woman wants to see you," he said.

I was confused—didn't know where I was. I looked around and remembered. I looked at the counter to see Kim shrugging on her coat and wrapping a scarf around her neck. I shuffled up to the counter.

"You're really hurting aren't you," she said with genuine concern.

"I'm alright," I lied.

"Look, I'm going home for dinner—why don't you come with me? We can talk."

I didn't want to seem too eager, but I still agreed rather quickly. I turned and looked at the guys. They were dozing or reading quietly. Only Brad was watching me with interest.

"Okay."

I followed Kim out the door into the night. She led me off the base and down some narrow streets before coming to a weathered green door. She unlocked it and we stepped in. It was a single room with a stone floor, stone walls, a fireplace in one corner, a small kitchen off to the side, and a bed in the middle. She closed the door and I felt a draft of cold air come through a very large crack at the bottom of the door.

"Sit down on the bed. I'll get the fire going."

I plopped down on the bed and watched Kim as she put chunks of olive wood onto the fire. She was a pretty woman in a subtle, understated way. She was dressed conservatively in fading blue jeans and a baggy sweater. Still, even that didn't conceal her full curves and bosom. As she bent over the fire I couldn't resist the way her jeans clung to her wide hips or the small curve of white skin that was exposed when she reached toward the fire. She had a feminine softness that, in that moment, I found desirable.

The fire popped and squealed as the bark caught and began to glow. Kim lit a burner on the stove and began boiling water for coffee. She came back over to me and stood before me.

"Take off your clothes."

I was too tired to be having thoughts of sex, but I could tell that wasn't what she meant anyway. I stripped out of my uniform with agonizing stiffness as she helped me. The cuts and scrapes on my body were healing, but they were still angry and painful. The deep cuts on my legs still oozed blood between the stitches and had soaked through the bandages.

"I have bandages in my bag," I said to her.

She opened it and pulled the small plastic bag from the top where I had placed tape, bandages, and medicine. She cut off the old bandages with scissors and gently wiped my wounds with a warm cloth before rebinding them in clean bandages. As I finished putting the strips of tape on Kim returned with a steaming mug of coffee and handed it to me. My skin was goose-pimpled from the creeping cold. Kim noticed and pulled back the covers on the bed. I needed no coaxing to crawl in. I leaned against the wall while Kim sat on the corner of the bed. I looked at her closely. Maybe it was her faith—if she still had any—but the lines on her face spoke of sincerity and honesty.

"Why would you help?" she asked. "You don't even know me."

"Because I can. Because people have helped me. Because it really requires nothing of me to help."

I was honest. New York was only a few hours away. I lived alone in a three bedroom house. It seemed like the right thing to do. She seemed like someone who deserved it. Certainly others had helped me out of scrapes when they had nothing to gain.

We talked more. We talked about where we were from, our families, our pasts. Nothing too serious. Nothing too painful. I finished my coffee as we spoke and fatigue swept over me. I slid down deeper into the covers. I remembered Kim smiling at me in amusement. I couldn't believe how tired I was. My head settled into the pillow and I slept.

At one point I felt a heavy cover of some kind, a large fur of sheepskin as it turned out, being pulled over me. I opened my eyes groggily and saw Kim standing over me, wearing her coat and scarf again.

"I have to go back in and finish my shift. You stay here and sleep. There's more coffee if you want some—but I think you should stay right there."

"Thanks," I said in a low, muffled voice as sleep marched over me again. I heard the door close and lock. For the first time in weeks I felt safe and I slept with a soundness that had eluded me for months.

About midnight I heard Kim come back in. I didn't really wake up, but heard her moving about and then felt the covers shift as she crawled in. I could smell her scent mixed with the cold outdoor air. I was aware of barely-warm, naked skin pressing up against me, soft breasts pressing into my back, and Kim's arm lying lightly around my side. Her breath fell warmly upon my neck and I slept once more.

I awakened to soft kisses brushing the nape of my neck. I felt wonderfully rested and opened my eyes to see narrow beams of sunlight streaking into the room from around the drawn curtains. The fire burned warmly and radiated throughout the room. Kim had obviously piled more wood on it in the early hours of the morning. Hands stroked slowly over my chest and lightly down over my stomach as the kisses roamed over my neck. Kim's body was spooned closely up to mine.

"Did you sleep well?" she asked in a voice as soft as her kisses.

"Mmmmm—god—yes. I haven't slept like this in months."

I also hadn't been in bed with a naked woman in nearly a year and one part of my body was already wide awake. Somehow, I think she already knew that.

"Do you mind? I mean, do you mind me doing this?"

"It's the nicest thing I've ever felt." I meant it.

I knew she wasn't doing this because of my promise to help her back to the States. I had already promised that—no conditions. That made this even better. We were just two lonely people thrust together by circumstance in a land where neither of us belonged, each of us longing for just a moment of closeness with another human.

Kim's fingers began to slip inside the snug waistband of my skivvies, her fingertips just barely brushing the tip of my cock. My cock twitched in anticipation. Kim's hand slipped deeper and her warmth enveloped my hard cock. I moaned. How could I not?

"Let's slip these off," she suggested as she began gently coaxing them down my battered legs and off over my ankles. She immediately took my cock tenderly in her hands and began to stroke the velvety soft skin. I was lost in sensations and aware of her body brushing and stroking against mine. I began to stroke her back with my hand as she nuzzled me. I had not been touched by a woman in nearly a year and every sexual nerve in my body was screaming at full alert.

Kim rolled carefully over on top of me, folding my cock upward so it lie nestled in the soft hair and flesh between her thighs. She lay down and pressed her lips to my chest, kissing me softly while clinging to my shoulders with her hands. She looked at me with sparkling blue eyes and raised her hips just enough to guide my cock into her body. She lowered herself, eyes closed, slowly down the length of my cock. I was delirious with pleasure and felt her warmth flow through my body. She leaned forward, pulling the covers over us, until her erect nipples dimpled my flesh and she began to move slowly and deliciously against my cock. The weight of her breasts caressed my skin as her movements became more hungry and urgent.

Kim's kisses stopped as she began to focus on the spreading pleasure at our centers. She bit her lip as she began to stroke deeply onto my cock. Our breathing became panting and groaning as our excitement built. Kim sat upright, throwing back the covers, and pressed her hands to her breasts. Her skin glowed in the warm light of the fire. Her hands seemed so tiny as they filled with the soft flesh. Her moans climbed and she began to pull her nipples and roll the firm, brown aureoles in her fingers. Her head was arched back, stretching the cords in her neck tightly, as her hips rocked fore and back in an attempt to devour the flesh inside her cunt. I gripped her about the waist and held her down tightly. I felt the cum begin to build, ready to erupt within her and with a loud groan I began to come ferociously. Wave after wave of pleasure swept over me as my salty cum spurted into her and just as quickly drained from her and over my balls. It only heightened the intensity of pleasure that framed Kim as she continued to fuck me harder and faster. One hand dived down between us and stroked her clit. As soon as her fingers touched that oh so sensitive pearl she exploded in an orgasm that shook our bodies and the bed itself. She shuddered and sat frozen upon me before flowing down, in slow motion, like a leaf settling to earth, to rest once again upon my chest, my cock still buried deep within her.

I was still aroused and could feel her cunt pulsing with her heart around my firm cock. In spite of the pain in my legs I rolled over on top of Kim without slipping out of her. Her eyes were still closed and as I pressed myself deeper she drew her legs up beside me, beckoning me deeper still. I began to gently stroke within her soft body, feeling her rise to meet my shallow thrusts. Her breathing matched our rhythm and each time I pressed deeper she moaned softly. I lowered my weight onto her and wrapped my arms around her head and shoulders, holding her tightly. I could feel my climax approaching quickly and Kim was coaxing me on, urging me to fill her again. Her arms wrapped around me, holding me close to her body as our hips thrust against one another. My cock swelled and shuddered as my cum once more flowed into her body. I was dizzy from the intensity. Kim's climax was a gentle, peaceful one and a relaxed expression and smile spread across her face. We lay motionless together, my cock softening within her and slowly creeping out of her.

I finally rolled off of Kim and wrapped my arms around her, my body curled behind hers. We drifted off to sleep again and I finally stirred when I felt her leave the bed in the early afternoon.

"I have to go to work," she said rather forlornly.

"Thank you," was the only thing I could think of to say.

She leaned over and kissed me.

"Come on down to the terminal when you're ready. Try to be there by late afternoon—there may be some flights available.

The door closed and I laid back into the bed, staring at the ceiling. After a few minutes I got up and dressed. I couldn't shower because of the bandages and, in a way, I was grateful because I could smell Kim's scent on me and I didn't want to wash it off just yet. Kim had left out some bread and fruit for me to eat and I munched on it as I boiled some coffee.

I walked into the terminal about 1700 and saw Kim behind the counter. She smiled at me and motioned me over.

"Let me see your orders," she said as she held out her hand. I passed them to her. She wrote some notes, crossing out some entries, and then handed them back to me.

"Your flight leaves in one hour—they're getting it ready now."

I could see a C141 out on the tarmac, being loaded with cargo. I looked at my men and Kim spoke.

"They're leaving too—on the same flight."

I knew Kim had something to do with arranging this. I looked at her as I would a good friend.

"Thank you."

I seemed to be saying that a lot lately. Kim's boss came over to her and spoke quietly. When he left she turned back to me.

"I have to leave now. I'm going to be working in a different building for a while. If I don't see you again, have a safe trip."

She looked at me for what seemed like a very long time without saying a word. I pulled a small piece of paper from my wallet and wrote my name and stateside telephone number on it. I pushed it towards her.

"Call me—I'll be there when you need me."

She held it in her hands then folded it and slipped it into her pocket. She leaned across the counter and gave me a small hug.

My men and I boarded the huge plane and settled into jump seats. A few minutes later the plane rumbled down the runway and lifted off for the fourteen hour flight back to the states. I thought we were flying to Philly—that's what the flight manifest in the terminal had said. After we were up to altitude I went into the cockpit to speak to the pilot about arrival times and destinations. I expected to have to arrange travel for my men to the base.

"What time do we land in Philly?" I asked the flight crew.

"We're not going to Philly—at least you're not."

"What do you mean?" I asked, more than a bit perplexed.

"Last minute change—the manifest was modified. We have one pallet out of the whole damn load that's going to Norfolk. Look's like it's your lucky day," he said with a grin.

I looked at the schedule in his hand and recognized Kim's name and writing—like that on my own orders. I knew luck had nothing to do with it. I went back and told my men that we would be home at 0700—home in Norfolk.

A couple of weeks later I had a collect telephone call from Spain. It was Kim. She had a one-way ticket and would be leaving in a week for JFK. I promised I would be there when she landed.

I was.

About the Authors

Angela Wallis—is an author of erotic short stories who often tries to experience in the real world what she writes or reads in erotic fantasies. Her admonishment to anyone who will listen is that it is better to treasure what you have done than to regret what you haven't. Known as the "brunette hunkette" to those who know her, Angela is twenty-something, unmarried, but with various personal entanglements. When she is not writing, reading, or experiencing erotica she is busy providing administrative, travel, and personal services to business executives.

"Selene"—is the pen name of a woman whose main occupation has until lately been that of a wife and mother, writing being an enjoyable pastime. This is her first published work of fiction.

Felecia Barbaro—lives in Brooklyn, New York. She graduated from Pace University with a BA in English and worked as an administrative assistant at a Wall Street bank for several years before quitting in 1999 to write full-time. Felecia is currently at work on her first novel, as well as several stories. This is the first professional appearance for her fiction.

L.M.H.—is a full time, undergraduate student of English and Criminology at the University of New Mexico. Her writing is inspired by her world—both real and fantasy.

Jason Charles—is the author of *Tree Frog* (Hamilton, London), an erotic crime novel. His PhD was a study in twentieth century American novelist E. L. Doctorow focusing popular history and literary genres. He has published a number of book reviews for a variety of academic journals. Jason is, at the time of publication, finishing his second crime novel *Keith*.

Ray Leaning—is the incredibly talented artist who designed the cover for this edition. Although he creates art for many commercial publications and marketing productions his real love is creating erotic images of women. More examples of his art can be found on his web site at www.leaning.co.uk.

Susan Van Scoyoc—is an English psychologist and writer living in London. She writes and publishes on women's issues and general psychology as well as erotica.

Stephen Van Scoyoc—is an American writer living in London. He writes on a number of topics including Romantic literature, crime thrillers, and erotica. He has recently published *Emily's Vengeance* and is now writing *Closet Desire III—The Erotic Mystery of Valldemossa*.

You are invited to visit the Closet Desire website at www.closetdesire.com